"I'm saying that I love you, Justin." Kate released his hand and traced the rough edge of his jaw with her fingertips. "And that I want you." She drew back just an inch, giving him a sideways look. "That is," she added, smiling, "if you're still interested."

His answer was a kiss, urgent and deep, sending a new, dangerous, intoxicating feeling to join the heady joy already bursting within her.

Slowly he lowered her to the sand. He kissed her again, and she heard herself moan softly. Kate let her hands roam over the hard ridges and curves of his body, smooth and sculpted as a dune. She knew it all so well, but this time he felt new to her. Each kiss tasted of adventure and joy and something sweet and pure that she knew was love.

She did love Justin, she always had, and she probably always would. And he loved her. She could see it in his tender smile, feel it in his touch. This was right for her. And from now on, she was doing what was right, for her, and only for her.

Don't miss any of the titles in the **making waves** series by Katherine Applegate

#1 *Making Waves*
#2 *Tease*
#3 *Sweet*
#4 *Thrill*
#5 *Heat*
#6 *Secret*
#7 *Attitude*
#8 *Burn*
#9 *Wild*
#10 *Chill*
#11 *Last Splash*

making waves

Tease

katherine applegate

17th Street Press
New York

For Michael, as always.
Couldn't have done it without you.

Published by
17th Street Press
an imprint of
17th Street Productions
an Alloy Online, Inc. company
151 West 26th Street
11th Floor
New York, NY 10011

Cover photography by Garry Wade/Stone.
Cover design by Lauren Monchik

ISBN: 1-931497-13-3

Manufactured in the United States of America

First 17th Street Press Books printing June 2001

Originally published by HarperCollins Publishers as *Ocean City: Love Shack*

10 9 8 7 6 5 4 3 2 1

one

"Come on, Kate, do something," Chelsea Lennox urged as she adjusted the zoom lens on her camcorder.

Kate Quinn glanced self-consciously at the nearby group of guys leering at her over sunglasses and noses thick with zinc oxide. It was early afternoon, and like most summer Sundays, the miles of Ocean City beaches were packed with sun worshipers. "Like what?"

"I don't know." Chelsea shrugged. "Don't just strike a pose. Do one of those supermodel moves where you kind of leap through the air and flail your arms around."

"Is that what people usually do on the beach? Leap and flail?"

"Search me," Chelsea said. "I've only been a beach photographer for a couple of hours, remember. My boss just told me the prices for still shots and videotapes. She didn't tell me what people were supposed to do."

They walked a few steps over the hot sand, threading their way through beach blankets while ignoring the occasional whistle or proposition from guys. The air shimmered before them, a white-hot oven relieved only by the occasional halfhearted breath of wind off the ocean's surface. The sand burned Kate's feet around the edges of her sandals.

Chelsea struggled to adjust the two black straps around her neck. "These cameras are heavy," she complained. "If I keep this job all summer, I'll have the neck of a fullback."

Kate smiled. Somehow the high-tech photo equipment didn't quite go with Chelsea's outfit—a purple tank top emblazoned with a glitter screen appliqué of a dragon and a floral-print wraparound skirt. Chelsea had designed the appliqué herself and applied the beads by hand.

"It's a definite improvement over your last couple of jobs," Kate said as she smoothly dodged a wayward Nerf ball. "You look like a real photographer."

"Uh-huh." Chelsea fiddled with a dial on the side of the camera. "I wonder what this thingy is, anyway? Come on, Kate, do something photogenic so I can practice. Think Victoria's Secret—toss your hair and pout."

"How about if we just forget it?" Kate suggested in a low voice. "I already feel like the whole beach is staring at us. And that's *without* any tossing or pouting."

"Oh, give me a break. You've got it, now flaunt it."

A trio of nearby guys hooted encouragingly. Kate grabbed Chelsea's arm and pulled her toward the edge of the water. "That does it. You're going to have to stick to paying customers. I'm just here to read a good book and get a little tan," she said.

Chelsea eyed Kate's bathing suit and cocked an eyebrow. "In that new suit you'll get more than a *little* tan, Kate. You'll get just about everything tan."

Kate tugged at the strap of her leopard-print bikini. It was a recent addition, bought on a whim last week at a little boardwalk store called Full Disclosure. She already had two great Speedo suits, sleek, comfortable maillots that were perfect for the long swims she liked to take over in the calmer waters of the bay. This suit, on the other hand, was perfect for standing very still and not making any sudden movements. "Is it too . . . you know?" Kate asked.

"Well, if what you were really doing is just lying out reading a book, it would be too . . . you know," Chelsea said, laughing. "But since I know what you're really going to do is lie out and read that book directly in front of Justin's chair, I don't think it's too . . . you know."

"Do you think Justin can see through me the way you can?" Kate asked.

"Sure. That's why you like him so much." Chelsea paused to train her still camera on a windsurfer skirting the shore, but just as she started to focus, the guy wiped out with a splash. "Not enough wind, I guess," she commented. "It's really still today." She let her camera fall to her side, where it swung lightly as she walked. "Do you think Connor can see through me the way you can?"

Kate grinned. "I don't suppose you're referring to the way you just happened to accidentally run into him in the upstairs hall yesterday?"

"That *was* an accident!" Chelsea protested.

"Uh-huh."

"There's nothing between Connor and me," Chelsea said firmly. She turned and gave Kate a sly grin. "Yet, anyway."

"Thought so."

"Besides, it'd never work, Kate," Chelsea continued. "I mean, he's Irish, I'm American. He's white, I'm black. He's a pain in the butt, I'm—" She grinned. "Okay, so we *do* have something in common. Still, I'm not so sure about going out with a guy I live with."

"I'm going out with Justin," Kate pointed out.

"Justin at least lives down in the boathouse. Connor and I share a wall." Chelsea sighed and looked away. She seemed to be about to say something, but then she stopped herself. "Well, I better get to work," she said at last. "There's a beach full of people wanting these magic memories preserved for all time, or at least until their VCR eats the tape." She took Kate's arm. "Come on. I'll walk on down with you. That way it won't look quite so obvious when you just happen to end up near his chair."

Justin's lifeguard chair was like all the others, placed every block or so along the beach—a whitewashed wood platform raised five feet off the ground. He was sitting back, scanning the beach, all the way left, then slowly all the way to the right. His dark hair spilled over the band of a white sun visor pulled low over his sunglasses. His deeply tanned shoulders and strong arms were visible above the rail of his perch.

Kate paused for a moment. Sometimes when she saw Justin, a hot, dizzy, delicious feeling washed through her, a realization of just how lucky she was to have this second chance to be with him. Last summer they'd blown it. But this summer would make up for everything. This summer was going to be perfect, and what happened after August, when she went off to college and he sailed off into the sunset, well . . . she'd worry about that when the time came.

"Wipe that silly grin off your face," Chelsea instructed.

Kate laughed. She had a tendency to do that around Justin these days. "He does look great in those red lifeguard trunks, doesn't he?" she whispered.

"You're not the only one who thinks so," Chelsea pointed out, nodding at the heavy concentration of pretty girls lounging on beach towels in Justin's immediate vicinity.

"Oh, so you see them, too. I thought I was just being paranoid," Kate said.

"Nope. But hey, that's life. Lifeguards attract girls. Good-looking lifeguards, especially."

Far out past the surf line, Kate noticed a beautiful sailboat, much larger than the compact boat Justin was laboring to restore. This was a real yacht. She looked over at Justin again. Not surprisingly, he was shooting glances at it between scans of the beach.

"Nice boat," Chelsea said.

Kate smiled to herself. Not a bad test. Could Justin actually tear his eyes away from the boat and the beach to look at her?

"Hi, Justin," she called out.

Justin lowered his gaze, then lowered his sunglasses. He smiled as his gray eyes met hers, then traveled down the length of her body. His next smile had a different element added to the warmth.

He climbed down from the chair and took her in his arms, careful, even as he held her, to keep his face turned toward the water. "How am I supposed to concentrate on my work when you show up looking like this?" he asked.

"It seemed to me you were concentrating on that sailboat," Kate pointed out.

"What sailboat?" he said huskily, kissing her deeply.

"There, that's what I'm looking for—action." Chelsea focused the camera on Kate and Justin.

"Beautiful," Justin murmured as he pulled away, his eyes on the water.

"It is, isn't it?" Kate said, staring out at the boat.

"Actually, I meant you."

Kate smiled. She'd heard it before from other guys. But she'd always suspected they were just seeing the outside Kate, the tall, blue-eyed blond, the golden girl with the easy smile. When Justin said she was beautiful, she really *felt* beautiful.

Suddenly a concussive explosion rocked the air. Justin tore himself free of Kate's embrace and scanned the water, cursing under his breath.

Kate followed the direction of his gaze. The sailboat was an island of flames and smoke in the surrounding sea.

Justin gave three short blasts on his whistle. Then he snatched up a red plastic buoy and slung its rope over his shoulder.

"Justin!" Kate cried. "Justin!"

But he was already out of earshot, swimming like a torpedo toward a pillar of smoke that rose in deadly billows toward a cheerful sun.

two

Justin was relieved to be beyond the worst of the breaking waves. Fighting them was tiring, and he couldn't afford to be worn out too quickly.

It was hard to keep his bearings. The surge and roll of the sea hid the boat from sight; all he could track on was the tower of smoke that rose high overhead. Justin knifed through the water, making every movement count. He was a strong swimmer, one of the fastest on the Beach Patrol, but even a second's delay could mean the difference between life and death.

A couple more strokes and the boat—what was left of it—came into view. The explosion had blown away the entire superstructure—the cabin, the mast, the deck. An oily fire was eating its way down to the waterline. Any second, what was left of the hull would disappear beneath the surface.

Justin swam to within a few yards of the

wreck, as close as he could get. There was something strangely unreal about the fire, raging away on the gentle swells. The heat was intense, blowing toward him like a torch. Every few seconds he had to duck his head under the water to cool off.

"Anybody there?" he shouted, his voice consumed by the roar of the flames.

He began to swim around the boat, passing by the bow. His eyes burned, and his throat was raw from the thick smoke. He shouted again, and this time he heard a desperate response.

"Help! Help us!"

Justin swam closer, braving the blistering heat until he couldn't take it any longer. He dove under the surface of the water. The hull floated above him, ringed by bright orange-and-yellow flame, but now the inferno was eerily silent.

Then he saw two sets of legs. A large man, wearing a pair of billowing black swim trunks, and beside him a small boy. The man was clearly foundering, and in a desperate attempt to save the boy, he had tied the trailing end of the bowline around the boy's waist. It had probably seemed like a good idea to a confused and frightened man, but Justin knew instantly that the rope might well mean the boy's death.

The man sank several feet before fighting his way clumsily back to the surface. Realizing the man was injured, Justin came up for air and swam furiously toward the wreck. The man lashed out in panic when Justin grabbed his shoulder, driving a powerful leg toward Justin's stomach. Justin evaded the blow, and the man seemed to come to his senses.

"Here." Justin thrust the buoy toward him. "Hang on to this."

"My son . . . ," the man gasped.

"I'll get him."

But at that moment the hull finally lost its last buoyancy, and with a loud, prolonged hiss that extinguished the flames and turned seawater to steam, it slipped below the surface. The rope around the drowning boy's waist straightened, then tightened. Justin saw just a flash of his face, eyes wide in horror as he was pulled underwater.

Justin sucked in a lungful of air and dived after the boy. It took all his power to match the speed of the sinking boat. With outstretched fingers he barely caught the tail end of the rope as it fluttered past. He held on tightly, letting it drag him toward the sandy bottom.

The drowning boy's eyes seemed to focus as he made out Justin's shadowy outline. He let out a scream that was muffled by the water.

Justin worked his way to the boy, tearing at the waterlogged knot that was almost impossible to budge. His lungs were burning from lack of air. His brain screamed for him to surface. The boy began thrashing desperately as his lungs filled with water, making Justin's task even more difficult.

Then the rope slipped an inch. Justin grabbed the loosened loop with his teeth and pulled. The knot came apart. But Justin was beginning to feel blackness close in around him.

More from training and instinct than from conscious thought, he passed his arm under the child's chin. The boy was motionless now, limp. Justin kicked his legs, aiming toward a faraway light, a light that seemed to be a million miles away.

It wasn't as if Kate didn't know what was happening. She felt the huge crowd pressing in at the water's edge. She heard their murmured questions. *What happened? Do you think anyone's still alive? Where did that lifeguard go?* She heard a siren in the distance. She saw two other lifeguards, Alec and Luis, swimming as hard as they could, converging on the spot where Justin had gone under. She even registered the pull of the wet sand on her toes as the waves continued their gentle, unconcerned teasing.

But then there had come that burst of steam, after which the smoke ceased and dissipated. Kate had realized with a shock that the flaming boat had been sucked beneath the water. After that there had been nothing, only featureless water and a single glimpse between rolling swells of a man clutching a red plastic buoy. She waited, motionless, not daring to blink for fear she'd miss seeing Justin, while the whole world seemed to hold its breath.

"There's a Beach Patrol boat," Chelsea said, pointing to the small white motorboat churning through the water.

Kate nodded slightly, her eyes still riveted on the area where Justin had disappeared.

"They don't know where to look," someone cried. People onshore were shouting and waving, trying to direct the rescue craft, but there was no way the lifeguards on board could hear. They didn't even seem to have spotted the man Kate had seen.

"Kate."

Kate felt Chelsea's hand on her shoulder.

"He's okay, Kate. Justin's a pro."

Kate didn't answer. She couldn't stand the waiting any longer. "I'm going in," she said firmly, but as she stepped toward the water, Chelsea grabbed her arm.

"Don't be a fool," she warned.

"I'm a strong swimmer," Kate growled, trying to shake off Chelsea's hand.

"It's a long way out there. That patrol boat will get to him long before you do. You don't want to get in the way and make things worse, do you?"

Somewhere in Kate's mind, she knew Chelsea was making sense, but this felt so wrong to her. She wasn't a bystander; she couldn't just stand here and wait. Shaking her legs restlessly, her whole body coiled and tensed, Kate clenched and unclenched her fists.

"He has to be okay," she whispered. "He has to be." But the rise and fall of the swells hid the little rescue boat from view.

"They're pulling someone out of the water," Chelsea said suddenly. "I saw them. It looks like . . ." She paused and looked over at Kate. "It's not Justin. It's an older guy. Oh, wait. There. Isn't that Justin?"

"I see him!" Kate cried. "It *is* him. I'm sure of it!" Of course, she couldn't be sure, but the person she'd glimpsed being hauled out of the water was wearing red lifeguard trunks. It *had* to be Justin. He had something limp and pale in his arms.

"He's not moving," someone in the crowd said.

"Please," Kate whispered. The boat raced

straight toward the beach, coming out of the swells and into view.

Then she saw it. A faint movement. A wave. Justin's wave.

Finally, at last, Kate let herself close her eyes.

The boat raced in toward shore just as a helicopter began a noisy descent onto the beach.

"The guards on the rescue boat must have radioed for help," Chelsea said.

When the boat made it to shore, paramedics leaped from the helicopter and began to treat the boy. The big man was whisked away on a stretcher. Justin stumbled a bit as he climbed out of the boat, but it was hard to tell whether that was because he was exhausted or simply because the huge crowd was swarming close to pat him on the back.

Kate didn't remember running to him. She only remembered holding him and vowing never to let him go.

three

Grace Caywood pulled her royal blue Eclipse into the parking place on the airfield and turned off the engine. As she stepped out of the car, she kicked an empty beer bottle from the floorboard onto the sizzling tarmac. She stooped down and tossed it into the backseat with the others.

Grace gazed up at the sky. The sun throbbed, hazy and indistinct, behind a gauzy layer of clouds. Despite the haze, the morning was turning into a scorcher.

This was a part of the airport Grace had never been to, far from the passenger terminal. Small one- and two-engine private planes and jets were parked on the tarmac around a large hangar that was badly in need of a new paint job.

She leaned against the hood of her car and watched as an old twin-engine Piper climbed slowly through the tissue of clouds. *That could be me soon*, she thought. If she could round up the nerve. Not to mention the money.

A smile came to her lips as she imagined soaring past her mother's ocean-side penthouse someday, giving her a tip of the wing as she buzzed by. Grace could practically hear her mother's horrified reaction. *Grace,* she would say, her voice soaked with fine scotch, *you have your choice of Ivy League schools. You have the beauty and brains to do whatever you want.*

But all Grace really wanted right now was to fly into the clouds and disappear.

"Hey, Grace. Over here."

Grace saw a head poke up from the far side of one of the planes. "David?"

"Come on over. See my baby."

Grace ducked under the wingtip of one plane and ran across the tarmac to a small, white single-engine plane. The engine's covering was raised, and David Jacobs leaned over it on a step stool, with a crescent wrench in his hand.

He smiled broadly at Grace, white teeth in a darkly unshaven face. "Hi. I'm glad you came."

Grace smiled back. David looked even better than she'd remembered. Especially this way—in formfitting jeans and no shirt. A trickle of sweat was making its way down his tanned chest, his hands were smudged with grease, and the back pocket of his jeans was hanging by a thread, but somehow on David the grease-monkey look was devastating.

"I'm glad I came, too," Grace said. She placed her hand against the warm steel of the plane's cowling. It was the first time she'd been this close to the small planes that she'd so often watched taking off from the Ocean City airport. "I assume *this* is your baby?"

David closed the cowling and climbed down the stepladder, wiping his hands on a rag. "Cessna 152. My baby."

"You told me you used to fly jets in the air force," Grace said. "Isn't this kind of—"

"Slow?" David completed her sentence, smiling ironically. He nodded. "Yeah, she's no F-15. She won't do Mach 2, and she won't be winning any dogfights, but there is one major advantage to my Cessna."

"What's that?"

"She's *my* Cessna. All mine. Unlike my F-15, which belonged to the American tax-payer." He finished wiping his hands and tossed the rag into his open toolbox. "So. You said you wanted to learn how to fly."

Grace nodded. "I told you I come out here and park at the end of the runway a couple of times a week. Whenever I'm feeling down or just need to think, I lie back and watch the planes take off, and it always makes me feel . . . peaceful, I guess is the best word." She smiled. "I know that's a cliché."

"Maybe so," David said with a smile. "But it's how most pilots feel. I don't know anyone who flies just for the money. Most do it simply because they love flying." He retrieved a blue cotton work shirt that had been draped over the wing and began pulling it on, smiling at her as he did.

Maybe it was just the way he was looking at her, his brown eyes a little too intent, asking just a few too many questions, but Grace suddenly felt a bit unsteady, and she wasn't used to that. More often than not, she was the one stepping over the prostrate bodies of guys swooning at her feet. David, she could tell, wasn't like that. Was it because he was older? Maybe. But she'd dated other guys in their twenties, and none of them had ever looked at her quite this way. Maybe that was it. David wasn't just *looking* at her. He was *thinking* about her, trying to figure her out. She wasn't sure she liked that. It made her feel vulnerable, and Grace liked being in charge.

Meeting David's eyes, Grace felt her cheeks heat up.

Blushing. Another thing she wasn't used to

doing around guys. "Um, how much do lessons cost?" she asked awkwardly. She felt uncomfortable, bringing up money.

David showed no awkwardness, though. "Eighty bucks a lesson."

Grace winced. "And how many lessons will I need before I can fly?"

"You can get a license to operate a single-engine plane like this after forty hours. But I'd strongly advise you to go for fifty or sixty hours. The more hours you have in the air, the less likely you are to screw up."

"So . . ." Grace calculated quickly in her head. "We're talking about five thousand dollars, total."

David nodded. "And then all you can do is fly yourself or friends in a single-engine plane. You won't be getting a job with United."

She didn't have to think about it. "I want to do it," Grace said firmly. She stuck out her hand, and David shook it. Suddenly she grinned as the realization hit her. "I'm going to learn to fly! When do we start?"

"How about right now?"

"Now?"

"Yes. But there's one other thing we have to get straight."

"And what's that?" Grace asked.

David hooked his thumbs in his pockets

and gave her a thoughtful look. "Flying is serious business. We don't do this unless you're going to do it right."

"Don't you lose business with this tough-guy attitude?" Grace asked.

David cocked an eyebrow. "Could be."

"I'm sorry," Grace said. "I shouldn't tease you. I know you're just concerned about the lives of your students."

"Naw," David said. "It's my plane I'm concerned about. When we're flying, I'm the teacher, you're the student, and you do exactly what I say. That way we stay alive and we don't break anything."

"Yes, sir," Grace said seriously, snapping a reasonable facsimile of a salute.

David made a back-and-forth motion with his hand. "Pretty weak salute, but we'll let it go for now. You go around and climb in on that side," he instructed, pointing. "The student rides on the left."

"Just like that? We're going to do it?" Grace asked hopefully.

"Just like that," David confirmed.

Grace did as he said, passing around the propeller and reaching up to open the narrow door. She climbed up and slid into the bucket seat. A moment later David entered from the other side and dropped into the right-hand seat.

"Okay," David said. "Start her up."

"What?"

"Just kidding. But pay attention to the sequence. You'll be doing this yourself soon."

Grace watched as he began the starting procedure.

"Remember," he said, "that engine out there is basically just like a car engine, with one difference. When a plane engine conks out, you don't just pull over to the side of the road and call a tow truck."

Grace nodded. She felt a rush of adrenaline, part fear, part excitement, and savored it. She loved the idea that this wasn't altogether safe, the feeling of being on the edge.

She had flown before, of course. Several times she'd visited her father, who'd moved to California after he and her mother had divorced three years ago. But this wasn't like flying the friendly skies, with complimentary peanuts and a movie you'd already seen on HBO. From the inside, the Cessna looked even smaller and more rickety than it had from the safety of the tarmac. It reminded her of an old Volkswagen except that instead of a steering wheel, there was a sort of half wheel on top of a stick that went backward and forward. David told her it was called the yoke.

He started the engine. It was loud enough

to make conversation difficult but a long way from the reassuringly full-throated roar of a commercial jet's engines. The propeller began to turn and quickly became a blur. The plane shuddered and jerked; then David released the brake and the Cessna rolled across the tarmac, between the other parked planes and past Grace's car.

David settled a radio headset onto his head. There was a small microphone positioned an inch away from his lips, and he spoke into it briefly. Then he placed a similar headset on Grace. She felt his fingers tangle in her hair. Then she heard his voice through the earphones.

"Before any takeoff or landing you have to contact the tower," he explained, his voice rendered mechanical and flat. "You need their permission because you can only have one plane at a time on the runway. When you have two planes, you have what's known as a crash. Usually followed by a major fireball. We try to avoid fireballs."

Grace laughed. She wasn't sure if he could hear her. The Cessna picked up speed and rolled toward the end of the runway, where David brought it to a stop.

Grace gazed down the long concrete runway. Someone was parked in a car at the far end, waiting to watch the Cessna take off.

Waiting, just as she had done so many times before, feeling wistful and jealous and exhilarated all at once. But she wasn't standing on the ground this time; she was the one inside the plane. She was the one headed for parts unknown. The realization filled her with a wave of pure happiness, like nothing she had felt in a long while.

David gave her a wink. Then he advanced the throttles and the Cessna leaped forward and began speeding down the runway. The rush pushed her body against the seat, and Grace realized she was holding her breath. Below them, the wheels rattled and bumped along the pavement. Then, suddenly, the noise was gone.

The ground fell away beneath them, then tilted as David pulled the Cessna into a climbing turn. Farther and farther below them the long, narrow stretch of Ocean City appeared until she could see it all, end to end.

Grace could make out the thousands of sunbathers stretched out along the shore, tiny, colorful dots against the golden sand. A rippling line of blue and white ran parallel to the beach, while out beyond lay the vastness of the Atlantic. When David pulled the Cessna through a long, lazy turn, she could see the bay side, the shore marked by jutting piers lined with cabin cruisers. Somewhere down along that bay was the house where she was now living.

They were out over the ocean now, and her eyes were drawn to a collection of vehicles pulled onto the sand right at the edge of the surf. Emergency lights were flashing. A drowning, maybe. She hoped vaguely it didn't involve Justin, but then, Justin could take care of himself.

Above the little plane, to her right, to her left, as far as she could see, was a thin veil of clouds. Soon they'd be blanketed in them, invisible and absolutely alone.

It was just as she'd known it would be. It made everything simple.

"Let's stay up here forever," she whispered. Instantly she felt embarrassed, but when she looked over at David, something in his smile told her he knew exactly what she meant.

four

"Here," Chelsea said that evening, handing Justin a cup of coffee. "Don't worry. I didn't make it."

Justin was sitting comfortably in the dilapidated La-Z-Boy in the living room with his feet up. "Thanks, Chels," he said. "For bringing it. And for not making it." He reached down and scratched his dog, Mooch, behind the ear. The dog was wearing a bandage on his head, the result of a recent run-in with a speedboat.

Alec came into the room, carrying a bag of Chee-tos. He sported Beach Patrol swim trunks like Justin's and had the same lean, muscular lifeguard build. "Luis says you should probably take a couple of days off," he reported as he knelt down next to Mooch and balanced a couple of Chee-tos on the dog's nose. "He said he's worried that after this, your ego might just explode and injure innocent people."

Justin laughed. "Uh-huh, a little *unpaid*

vacation. The boss is such a sweetheart." He took a sip of coffee.

"You *should* take some time off," Kate said.

It was practically the first time Kate had spoken since they'd gotten home. Chelsea glanced over at her. She was leaning against the wall, arms crossed, rocking slowly back and forth. Kate had seemed preoccupied ever since they'd gotten home, but Chelsea figured that was only natural. She'd had quite a scare.

"So, how long does the period of hero worship generally go on?" Connor asked, coming in from the hall. He was wearing a dusty, torn T-shirt, dirty jeans, and muddy boots. His bleached-out curls were flattened from the hard hat he had worn all day. "A day? A week? A month?"

Justin laughed. "You made the coffee, right? That's plenty."

"What's with that outfit?" Grace asked, looking Connor up and down.

"I got a new job working construction for Halloran Company," Connor said. "We're building a Taco Bell. It's dusty, dirty work, but I console myself with the knowledge that the world will be a much better place with one more Taco Bell."

"What happened to you making doughnuts?" Grace asked.

Connor shot Chelsea a secret look. "This job pays better," he said. "And the hours are better. This way I have my nights off."

Chelsea knew that the real reason Connor had switched jobs was that he was working in the United States illegally. The Immigration Department had investigated O'Doul's O'Donuts, the place where he'd been working, and Connor, as well as several other Irish illegals, had been forced to find other employment. Chelsea had kept Connor's secret, even from Kate.

"Well, anyway, I thought you were amazing, Justin," Chelsea said. "But you scared us all to death."

"I scared *myself* to death," Justin admitted.

"The problem with you, Justin," Grace said, sauntering over and sitting on the arm of his chair, "is that you think you're immortal." She tousled his hair affectionately.

Chelsea watched the smile that passed between Justin and Grace. Yes, there was still that look in his eyes. Hard to define. Just a little . . . something. Well, that was inevitable. They had been friends for a long time. And more than friends for a while, at least.

Besides, Chelsea suspected Grace had that effect on most guys. She'd seen more than a few go into cardiac arrest after a passing nod from Grace. Maybe it was those green almond eyes. Or that mysterious half smile.

Chelsea wished she had a little more of Grace's sexy sophistication and a little less of that look that made grandmothers cry out, "She's so *cute!*" But there it was, her cross to bear. She was undeniably, unrelentingly, terminally *cute.* She was petite and curvy with a great big smile and great big brown doe eyes like a character in a Disney movie. She sighed to herself. That's what she was. An African American Bambi.

The phone rang, and Alec ran to get it.

"Alec, no!" Kate yelled. "It could be my parents."

But the receiver was already off the hook. Alec held it to his ear and in a high falsetto answered, "Hello? Who's calling, please?" He put the receiver to his chest and in his own low, masculine voice said, "Kate? It's your mom."

"Alec," Kate pleaded in a whisper, "can we just let the girls answer the phone, please? Just a little while longer, okay?"

Alec looked offended. "Are you saying that wasn't a perfectly good female voice?"

Chelsea sent Kate a sympathetic smile. Mr. and Mrs. Quinn were very nice, but Kate hadn't figured out a way to tell them that she was living in a house with three roommates of the *male* persuasion.

"Want me to run interference?" Chelsea volunteered. "You don't seem like you're up for a run-in with the folks."

"I can handle it," Kate said as she headed for the hall. "But thanks."

"Well, I'm off to the market," Connor announced in a muted voice that wouldn't be picked up by the phone. "Can I get anything for anyone else?"

"Get me some chips," Grace said. "I'll pay you when you get back. Plain potato chips. Not those blue things Alec bought last time."

"Right. I'm off, then," Connor said, pausing at the door. He glanced over his shoulder, raking his fingers through his long hair, an uncharacteristically self-conscious gesture that Chelsea found very sweet. She met his eyes, and he gave her that one-side-of-his-mouth grin that she also found very sweet. Then he shrugged. "Well, then," he said, still not budging.

"Um, I need a bunch of stuff," Chelsea said suddenly. She'd just gone to the grocery store yesterday, but she was sure there was something she needed. Milk. OJ. Something. "I think I'll go with you, if that's all right."

"Glad of the company," Connor said warmly.

Chelsea went to grab her purse. She passed

Kate in the hallway, slumped on the floor next to the telephone, rubbing her eyes and nodding methodically.

"I'm going to the store with Connor," Chelsea whispered.

Kate waved.

"You okay?" Chelsea asked.

Kate covered the receiver with her hand. "Me? Sure. Just . . . I don't know. Drained, I guess." She jerked her head toward the living room. "Have fun."

"Always do," Chelsea replied.

As she was leaving, she could hear Kate in the hallway, talking to her mom in a singsong voice.

"No, Mom," Kate was saying, "everything's fine. Don't worry about me, please. Everything's perfect. Everything's absolutely perfect."

The minimarket was only a few blocks from the house down the main boulevard that bisected Ocean City. Since neither Chelsea nor Connor had a car, they decided to walk. And since neither of them was in any real hurry to get to the market, they decided to take the long route along the boardwalk. When it came time to turn off for the market, though, Chelsea pretended she hadn't noticed. She was pleased when Connor glanced at the street sign and kept right on walking.

The crowds had thinned a bit since it was a Sunday, and most of the tourists were lining up outside dinner places with names like The Fisherman's Net or Captain Tony's All-U-Can-Eat Buffet. A few stragglers were still staked out on the beach, but it was largely deserted. Only the footprints in the sand and the occasional candy wrapper or plastic cup betrayed the fact that a few hours earlier the beach had been a writhing mass of prostrate humans. This time of day the gulls restaked their claim, and you could actually hear the rhythmic, steady pulse of the sea.

It was muggy out, the air thick and hazy, but the strange air made for the start of a killer sunset, a rough-textured canvas that spread high overhead from the direction of the bay and bled paler oranges and yellows into the deepening gloom over the ocean. "It's going to be a great sunset," Chelsea said, stopping to check out the sky. "I'd almost like to paint that."

"Why almost?"

"Sunsets are kind of corny as paintings. Besides, I don't do many landscapes," Chelsea explained. "Mostly I see myself doing very abstract stuff down the road. Of course, first you have to hone your basic drawing techniques and learn to handle your materials."

"You sound serious about it," Connor observed.

"I'm going to college in a few months. My art professors are going to be serious as heart attacks," Chelsea joked. "Besides, I want to enjoy making art, so I want to be able not to worry about unimportant things like grades and tests."

"Yes, I've mostly managed to avoid worrying about those things myself," Connor said.

"Did you ever think about going to school for your writing?"

He shrugged. "Thought about it. I ran away to America instead. Besides, *poeta nascitur, non fit*. Latin. It means a poet is born, not made."

They continued walking, a little slower, a little closer, and lapsed again into a comfortable silence. It surprised Chelsea that she didn't feel the need to fill the holes with talk. Usually she was the first person to leap into a conversational void. Quiet made her nervous.

It was nice that Connor seemed to understand her art. Greg, her last boyfriend, never had. He'd thought it was a cute little hobby, like macramé or needlepoint, not a potential career. And as for the guys she'd dated before that, she couldn't remember the subject ever even coming up. Still, maybe that was her fault. She'd spent plenty of hours admiring the rebuilt engine in Max's Corvette. She'd waxed positively poetic watching Thomas designing Web pages from scratch. But she'd never really expected them to reciprocate, to want to know about her life. She'd been satisfied with the fact that Kareem had those puppy-dog brown eyes you could practically swim laps in or that Joseph had that gravelly deejay voice that had made her toes tingle.

Chelsea was constantly falling victim to infatuations. She fell in love instantly and with complete conviction. And if things hadn't generally worked out too well, maybe it was partly her fault. The truth was, Greg had been a real marathon relationship for her—all of six months. She'd finally gotten up the nerve to tell him he couldn't control her life, but the more she thought about it, the more she was beginning to realize that she'd let him do it, just to avoid confrontations. She hated confrontations.

"Did you get any of this afternoon's events on tape?" Connor asked, breaking into her thoughts.

"Nope. Like an idiot, I was too busy being worried. I guess that means I'm not really cut out to be a news photographer."

"Justin is your friend," Connor said. "I think I'd be a little shocked if you could have remained indifferent."

"You, shocked?" Chelsea asked. "I never figured you as a guy who was easily shocked."

Connor laughed appreciatively. "So," he said, a sound he pronounced "soo." "How do you like the new job?"

"It's all right, I guess. Today wasn't exactly a fair test." She looked up at him. "How about your job?"

"It's bloody hard work," he said with a laugh. "But it's better than making doughnuts. I get to work out in the sun and fresh air. Plus I'm getting good honest calluses on my hands."

He paused in front of a little sunglasses store called Great X-Spec-Tations and held out his hand for inspection. Chelsea reached over and stroked his palm with the fingertips of her right hand. His skin was rough and warm. Without meeting his eyes, she let her fingertips linger, until a moment later his hand closed around hers.

They started walking again then, as if nothing had happened, as if nothing had changed between them. Chelsea concentrated on her feet, watching her red flip-flops snap against the sandy uneven boards as she tried to keep step with Connor's long, measured strides in his worn, heavy-soled work boots. But it wasn't really her feet she was thinking about. It was her right hand. Her fingers, her palm, her entire right arm were tingling with magical electricity.

Chelsea gulped and tried to think of something to say. "I liked it that you brought home doughnuts, though."

"What?" Connor asked, sounding a bit flustered.

"You know. When you made doughnuts and you'd bring a dozen home. Now all you can bring home is wood or something. Nails. Whatever."

"Oh. Yes. Right."

Amazing. Connor, actually at a loss for words? Usually it was hard to shut him up. If she didn't know better, she'd swear he was acting shy.

They kept walking at the same brisk pace, past a series of arcades, past the Believe-It-or-Not Museum, past the guy putting the finishing touches on his sand sculpture of the Last Supper. And still they kept holding hands.

It was such a simple, innocent gesture. The first guy she'd held hands with had been Terrence Dreyer, who, she later learned, had held hands with just about every eligible third-grade female at Shady Springs Elementary. A regular third-grade Romeo. The point was, she'd done it zillions of times since then. It didn't mean anything, really. So how did you explain this megawatt glow?

She looked down at their intertwined fingers. Odd, the way they made a pattern of black and white. It was the first time she'd ever held hands with a white guy. The first time she'd ever really wanted to.

She sneaked a glance at Connor. She liked the strong, hard angles and planes of his face, the deep-set hazel eyes that always seemed to be laughing at some private joke. Black, white, or green, he was a great-looking guy.

Still, all her boyfriends had been black, from Terrence all the way through Greg. Greg, who'd been wealthy and gorgeous and on his way to great things. All in all, a much better prospect than Connor, an illegal alien who might be shipped off to Ireland at any moment.

She wondered if Connor was silently remarking on the fact that he was holding hands with a black girl. Hopefully he was just thinking about the fact that he was holding hands with this girl named Chelsea, this girl whom he really liked. Hopefully he wasn't thinking of her as this *black* girl named Chelsea.

But then, she was thinking of him as this *white* guy named Connor, wasn't she? This very funny, very deep, very nice guy . . . *white* guy . . . named Connor.

"I, uh . . . I guess we'd better head to the market before it closes," Connor said.

Chelsea nodded. "Yeah, you're white." Instantly she realized what she'd said and stopped, covering her eyes with her free hand. "I mean, you're *right. Right!*"

Connor nodded as a slow grin spread across his face. "Yes, and *white,* too. Irish is as white as you can get, excepting a Swede or Norwegian, maybe. Does it bother you?"

"That you're white?" Chelsea said. "No. I mean, all we're doing is holding hands."

"True enough. Do you want to stop? Holding hands, I mean."

Chelsea shook her head and looked down, biting her lip. "No."

"Me neither," Connor said. "Then that's settled. Off to the market. Grace will be wanting her chips when we get . . . *black.*"

"Very funny, Connor," Chelsea said, poking him in the ribs. "Very funny."

five

Grace scooped up the American Express receipt from the table and glanced at the line where the tip was written in. A twelve-dollar tip on a sixty-eight-dollar check. Not bad. It was more than fifteen percent, although less than the twenty percent Grace looked for.

It was her last table of a very busy night. A surprisingly busy night for The Claw, given that it was a Sunday. There had been some sort of trade show over at the convention center and that tended to bring in a lot of good-tipping businessmen.

Grace had been working at The Claw since graduation, and so far she had nothing to complain about. Waiting tables wasn't exactly a fast-track job, as her mother had so often pointed out, but the money was pretty good, and Grace liked her fellow workers. The view wasn't bad, either. The Claw sat on the boardwalk. The downstairs was a bar and club, while upstairs was a white-tablecloth restaurant with wall-to-wall windows that gave an unobstructed view of the beach.

"They gone?"

Grace nodded to the busboy. "Yep, and I will be, too, in about five minutes."

She went to the cashier, who paid out all of Grace's charge-card tips, then headed toward the bar. The small bar was devoid of customers, all of them having moved to the club downstairs.

Anton, the bartender, busied himself behind the teak bar, wiping down the liquor bottles. Two other waiters were counting out their tips. Grace sat down on one of the bar stools and joined them.

Ten percent of her tips went to Anton and another ten percent to the bus dogs, as the bus help was affectionately known. The remaining eighty percent was hers. It came to ninety-eight dollars.

"Jeez, you had a good night," Anton said as she handed him a ten-dollar bill.

"I'm walking with almost a hundred," Grace admitted.

"You're taking home a buck on a Sunday?" Mike, the headwaiter, groaned, shaking his head. "I let them make me headwaiter because I thought *I'd* make all the money. I'm walking ··th seventy."

"Yeah, well, you don't have it goin' on the way she does." George, another waiter, winked at Grace and went back to making neat piles of quarters.

"You sexist," Grace said with a derisive laugh. "I made more because I turned more tables. If you'd stop wasting your time trying to pick up every female in your station, you'd go home with more cash."

"Yeah, but I'd never get a date."

"You don't get any now," Mike pointed out.

"You children want your shift drink?" Anton asked. "I'm getting ready to finish breaking down the bar."

The management at The Claw allowed their waiters a free drink at the end of each shift. It wasn't exactly legal, especially since several of the waiters were, like Grace, underage, but since the waiters usually managed to sneak a drink, anyway, many restaurants quietly tolerated a drink a night for their crews. Of course, as Grace knew well, there were many other ways to sneak booze—finishing the drink of a customer who'd left a little or placing phony drink orders that sneaked past the prying eyes of managers. She'd also learned to ply extra drinks out of Anton, who, like many bartenders, made much of his income from the waiters' tips.

"Let me have a peppermint schnapps," Grace said. "I have a date tonight." Peppermint schnapps tasted a lot like mouthwash. If anyone smelled it on her breath, there was a good chance they'd just assume it was a mint.

She tossed the drink down in a single gulp while Mike and George sipped their own drinks from white coffee mugs. The mugs were to fake out any end-of-night customers who might happen by the bar.

"Date?" Anton asked. "The flyboy you've been talking about all night?"

"His name's David," Grace said.

"I dated a guy named David once," Anton said, reminiscing.

"Not the same guy," Grace said with a smile.

"Don't be so sure," Anton persisted.

The door leading to the club downstairs opened, and a mixture of raucous laughter and jazz filled the air. Grace looked over and saw David, dressed in a worn leather jacket, jeans, and a dark T-shirt. He waved.

"Not the same David," Anton admitted. "*Him* I would definitely remember."

"Hi, Grace," David said. "Are you ready to go?"

"I still have some side work to do," Grace said, apologizing. "I have to fold napkins."

Mike hesitated, then made a brushing-away gesture. "Take off. Far be it from me to stand in the way of true love. Give me an extra five and I'll bribe the bus dogs to do it."

Grace handed him a five-dollar bill with a grateful smile and ran to meet David. They headed downstairs and out onto the boardwalk; Grace felt instantly revitalized. She yanked off her retro-print tie and undid the top couple of buttons of her white dress shirt. The tang of ocean air replaced the tired smell of stale beer and cigarette smoke in the restaurant. The night sky overhead was washed out by the neon fluorescence of the boardwalk, but out over the water the stars returned, bright and hard.

"My feet are killing me," Grace said. "Let's get off these boards."

She sat on the edge of the boardwalk, took off her black leather Reebok sneakers without bothering to untie them, and shoved them into her already overcrowded canvas bag. The sand was deliciously cool on her feet. David followed her example, shoving a loafer into each of the pockets of his jacket.

"Better, much better," Grace said.

"How was work?" David asked.

"Let's not talk about it. How's that for an answer?"

David laughed softly. "I guess that says it all."

They started across the sand, leaving

behind the ribbon of light from the boardwalk. Walking along slowly, they headed toward the edge of the water. The half-moon was haloed in clouds, but it shed enough light to turn the foaming wave crests luminescent. "This isn't my business," David said suddenly. "So don't answer if you don't want to, but you and Justin. Were you . . . ? I mean, that day at that stupid Beach Body Hottie Contest or whatever it was called, I thought I detected some chemistry between the two of you."

Grace took his arm. Beneath the cracked leather of his jacket she could feel his hard muscles. "Yes, we were. But that's all over now. It's been over for a while. Now it's him and Kate."

"The blond one, right?"

Grace nodded.

"Doesn't that make things a little . . . tense?"

Grace sighed. "I'm not feeling tense right now." As a matter of fact, that last shot of booze was beginning to take effect. It made for a nice, calming little buzz, along with the moonlight and the soft shushing of the surf advancing and retreating across the sand.

"Do you know the stars?" David asked.

"I've looked at them often enough," Grace said. "I suppose I should."

David paused near the water's edge and stared up at the sky. "Me neither. We had a course in astronomy at the Air Force Academy, but it's like most of what you learn in school. Quickly forgotten. The stuff I remembered all had to do with flying. Flying and fighting. How to pull out of an uncontrolled spin, how to lead a target with my guns, how to . . ."

He fell silent, and Grace waited patiently. She felt good, with that sweet warmth from the liquor bubbling through her veins. She didn't want to talk. Didn't need to. Let David do all the talking.

"Most of that is pretty useless now. I won't be doing a lot of dogfighting in my little Cessna," David finally continued dryly. "Just goes to show that what you think is important doesn't always turn out to be that way over the long run. Right now, right this minute, I'd rather know the names of those stars."

Grace waited, wondering if he would now tell her why he was no longer happily flying his jet. Why he was reduced to teaching flying lessons in Ocean City. When they'd first met, he'd told her it was a long story, one he would tell her someday. But he guarded his silence, content to gaze out at the stars.

A large wave crashed and washed over their toes before they could back away. It pulled the sand from under their feet as it retreated.

"That felt good," Grace said.

She felt David's arm slip around her waist and draw her close. His dark eyes glittered with moonlight and reflections of the faraway colors of the boardwalk. "This will feel better," he said gently.

He kissed her, holding her close against his chest. Grace saw the stars swirling overhead, then closed her eyes and kissed him back. It was better than she'd dreamed, so sweet and gentle that she found herself leaning forward hungrily, wanting more. She slipped her hands inside his jacket and ran her fingers over the hard heat of his chest.

Slowly, gently, David pulled away. He was staring at her with that same intrigued look he'd had at the airport that morning.

"What's the matter?" she asked.

"Peppermint schnapps," David said. Then he laughed a little uncertainly. "I remember the taste. Peppermint schnapps."

Grace felt her cheeks blaze. "I had a drink before I left work," she admitted, feeling a little embarrassed and confused. "We all did."

David nodded. "I know. It's nothing. Forget it." He shook his head. "It just surprised me."

"Well, you surprised me, too," Grace said. "I didn't know you were going to kiss me."

David pulled her close again. "Liar. You

knew I've been thinking of nothing else since I met you. You knew I couldn't wait to kiss you."

Grace raised herself on tiptoes and took his face in her hands. "Then don't wait any longer."

six

"Okay, now put the three-eighths socket on the socket wrench and hand it to me."

Kate stared blankly down at the toolbox, a collection of stainless-steel pieces in differing sizes and shapes that meant almost nothing to her. She glanced over at Justin. Or, more accurately, at Justin's legs, sticking out from under a low bench in the tiny area he thought of as the kitchen on his sailboat. *Galley,* she reminded herself.

"Give me a hint," she said with a sigh.

"Little round thing with notches inside that . . . never mind." He slid himself back out from under the bench and shook his head at her. "You're not my first choice as a carpenter's assistant, you know."

She leaned down and gave him a hand, pulling him to his feet. He brushed sawdust from his chest.

"Sorry," Kate said. "I could have found it in an hour or so."

"Come on. I've done enough work for tonight," Justin said. He snapped off the bare lightbulb that hung from an orange extension cord, and they climbed out of the cramped cabin onto the boat's deck.

They were inside the boathouse, a wooden structure with catwalks on both sides and a barnlike roof of bare beams overhead. Behind them, on the landward side of the boathouse, was a loft, open and guarded only by a single railing. A narrow wood staircase led up to it, a low, drafty space with just enough room for Justin's bed.

Kate looked along the length of the boat, beyond the bow, which pointed out toward the black water of the bay. With the boathouse gates open, it was easy to imagine the day when Justin would push his boat out onto the open water, raise sail, and head for the open sea. The thought filled her with a sudden wave of melancholy, a feeling she'd been battling off and on all day.

Justin pulled the ropes that swung the gate shut, closing out the night. She climbed off the boat onto the catwalk, carefully stepping over the boards and scattered power tools he had there.

Justin saw her looking toward his loft. "Come on up," he said, taking her hand. His palm was warm and calloused. "I promise I'll let you leave . . . eventually."

Kate followed him to the middle of the loft, where the roof was highest. There wasn't room for much, only the bed, a small dresser, and a rope strung between two rafters that served as a closet pole for Justin's few hanger-worthy clothes.

"Have a seat," he offered. He reached into a cooler half filled with slushy ice and pulled out two soft drinks. "You have a choice. Coke or Coke."

"How about a Coke?" she said, taking the can from his hand.

Justin sat on the bed, swinging his feet up and leaning against the wall. "Sit down," he said. "I think we need to talk."

"Usually that's the last thing you want to do when I come up here," Kate said, perching on the edge of the bed.

"I'm just wondering what's going on with you," Justin said gently. "You've been a million miles away ever since . . . the rescue."

Kate stared at the two tattered posters on Justin's wall. One was a sailboat. The other was a travel poster of lush Tahitian beaches populated by lush Tahitian women.

"That might as well be a million miles away," she said, pointing with her can at the travel poster. "Is that your first destination?"

"Could be."

"Gee, I can't imagine why," she said dryly.

He laughed. "You know, if you came along, I wouldn't even be tempted to look at those women."

Kate tried a smile, but it died on her lips. "It's not exactly safe wandering around out in the ocean in a little sailboat."

"I never said it was," he pointed out reasonably. "Look at what happened to that fool this morning. Of course, he probably let gas accumulate in his bilges or left the valve on his stove open."

"Look what almost happened to *you* this morning," Kate said, surprising herself with her sudden vehemence. She looked down at the floor, concentrating on one of Mooch's well-chewed rubber bones. "You could have been killed."

"I wasn't."

"You could have been," she persisted.

She heard him sigh. "I know this is a cliché, Kate, but I could get hit by a bus, too. Besides, from what you've told me, you've done a few dumb, dangerous things in your life. I mean, white-water canoeing? Scuba diving in an underground lake?

She acknowledged his point with a

shrug. "And if anything ever happened to me, my parents probably wouldn't know how to go on. After my sister died . . . after she . . ."

She still hated to say the words. *Committed suicide.* People heard it and instantly assumed Juliana must have been crazy, and Kate couldn't bear for anyone to think such a thing about her beautiful and brilliant older sister.

Of course, Justin knew about Juliana. Kate had told him about her last summer. But they'd rarely spoken about the suicide since, not because Justin wasn't ready to listen, but because Kate wasn't ready to talk.

"So, why do you go and do dangerous things?" Justin asked.

"I don't, not anymore." Kate watched the water bead on the side of her soda can, hoping Justin would let the subject drop. Instead he just sat there on the bed, arms crossed over his chest, waiting patiently for her to go on.

"I think I just pushed the limits for a while as a sort of rebellion," Kate said after a while. "You know, because my parents tried so hard to shield me. But then I realized that they had every right to feel protective over me."

Justin said nothing, silently signaling his disagreement.

"They were afraid of losing me. The same way I'm afraid of losing you."

He came closer and put his arm around her shoulders. "First of all, you're tougher than that. You got over your sister's death—"

"I did not," Kate interrupted. "I haven't forgotten Juliana."

"I didn't say forgot. I said you got over it, dealt with it. You have no choice in life but to get over losses."

"Like you and your father?" She said it angrily and was instantly sorry. Justin's father had walked out on Justin and his mother when Justin was nine years old, and they hadn't heard from him since.

Justin didn't seem at all offended. He just nodded. "Yeah," he said, stroking her arm, "exactly like me and my father."

She surprised herself by kissing him. He returned her kiss deeply, fiercely, holding her tightly. When they finally separated, neither spoke for a few minutes.

Finally Kate broke the silence. "You scared me, Justin," she whispered. "I suddenly had to face what life would be like without you, not at some indefinite point in the future, but right now."

"Right now is tough enough to handle without getting into a lot of what-ifs. Don't forget, our relationship was already dead and buried once. Neither of us thought we'd be together again."

Kate kissed him once more. They'd talked enough, and they weren't getting anywhere, anyway. "It's late, and I have to go to work in the morning."

"You could stay here," Justin said. He wasn't pleading or pressuring, just making a simple statement of fact.

"Justin—"

"I just meant that I thought you might like a little company tonight."

Kate looked at him doubtfully.

"Well, okay, I was ninety-eight percent sincere," he admitted. "But you already know that whatever you decide to do, I'll love you no matter what." He brushed her lips with a featherlight kiss. "There's no rush, Kate. We have plenty of time."

He was being sweet, trying to say all the right things, except that he'd just said the wrong thing. Maybe they didn't have plenty of time. That was the whole point.

She thought of her sister again. She thought of the terror she'd felt that morning, realizing she might have lost Justin. If she got any closer to him, wouldn't that make losing him all the more difficult?

"I'm going now," she said softly.

Justin followed her downstairs and kissed her one last time. "Know what?" he asked.

"What?"

"I really love you, Kate Quinn."

"I love you, too," she whispered back.

Maybe too much, she added to herself as she stepped into the warm embrace of the evening breeze.

seven

"Sir, could you please have your children use the rest room, not the ocean?" Alec asked calmly.

The tourist, a middle-aged man dressed in a bathing suit and green golf shirt, put his hands on his hips and gave Alec a look he'd seen plenty of times before, the one that said, *I'm old enough to be your father.*

"Where do you think the sewage goes in the end?" the man demanded, scratching at the thick layer of zinc oxide coating his nose. "What's the difference if my kid just cuts out the middleman, so to speak?"

Alec had to stifle the urge to laugh. There were parts of this job that were just plain ludicrous. "Sir, there is a city ordinance against cutting out the middleman, so to speak."

"Like my kid's the first one to pee in the ocean?"

"Sir, your son was . . ." Alec searched for a

discreet word, but nothing in his Beach Patrol training manual had prepared him for a conversation like this. "Sir, your son was *not* just peeing." Alec cleared his throat. "There are rest rooms up on the boards."

He climbed back up into his chair, careful as always to keep his eyes on the ball. Justin had warned him about working the south end of town. Even on a lazy Monday it was a zoo. Everywhere he looked, he saw trouble. Little kids with dime-store inner tubes, junior high hotshots on body boards, old folks who looked like they'd snap in two if a wave hit them wrong. Luis Salgado, the Beach Patrol lieutenant in this area, had decided last week to move Alec down to this end permanently. A promotion of sorts, he'd told Alec. What a con.

Now Alec was just a bit down from Justin, two hundred yards, to be exact. Not that they ever spoke. The only communication they had while on the job was through whistle signals and the occasional semaphore, a code that used two flags held in different positions to spell out words. It wasn't an easy way to shoot the breeze.

"Great." Alec groaned. While he'd been busy toilet training the tourists, someone had slipped into his zone with a surfboard. He'd been stopping surfers all morning. A tropical storm brewing out in the middle of the Atlantic was kicking up the surf, and waves were cresting a lot higher than usual. The south-end guards had been instructed to send all surfers up to the less crowded beaches on the north end of town. O.C. catered to families, Luis had explained, and parents had a tendency to get upset when their kids got bopped on the head by wayward surfboards.

Alec stood up on his chair and whistled sharply. The surfer either didn't hear or didn't care.

"Don't make me come get you, sucker," Alec muttered.

The surfer swung into position and caught a swell. He rode it inexpertly for a dozen yards before he fell backward. The board shot through the water several feet, narrowly missing a preteen girl who had tried out her flirting skills on Alec earlier that morning.

The surfer reeled his board back on its tether and paddled out for more. Alec whistled again. Still no response. What a piece of work.

He glanced for an instant over his shoulder. Justin had heard the whistle and gave Alec a go-ahead wave. Their sergeant was already gunning his four-by-four ATV toward Alec's stand so he could take over while Alec hit the water.

Alec jumped down out of the chair, slinging

his red buoy over his shoulder, and powered into the surf. It took only a few seconds for him to reach the surfer. "Hey, you!" Alec yelled. "I whistled you in, dude."

The kid grinned and gave him a raised middle finger. As he started to paddle away, a wave caught Alec unprepared and threw him back, allowing the kid to escape.

"Okay, now I'm going to bust him," Alec vowed. He kicked sharply to rise in the water and tried to spot the surfer.

He spotted him, all right. But too late.

The board was flying at him like an arrow. It hit him in the ribs with the force of a sledgehammer. Stopped suddenly by the impact with Alec, the surfer flew off the board. He and Alec tumbled helplessly in the wave as it deposited them near the shore.

Alec spit out a mouthful of water and rose vengefully from the retreating wave. At least, he *tried* to rise. The pain that shot through his side sent him sinking back to his knees.

"Take it easy, man. You got popped good." It was Justin, bending over him and helping him to his feet.

"Get that little—" Alec pointed in the general direction of the surfer.

"Don't worry. Luis has him. Can you walk?"

Alec tried a step. "Yeah, but my ribs feel like I got hit by a car."

"You may have cracked one. I've had that happen. Although it's probably just a little bruise. Either way it hurts."

"No kidding," Alec said sarcastically.

"Major ouchie. You want me to kiss it and make it better?"

"No, it's enough just to have a huge hero like you around in my hour of need."

Justin yelled over to Luis, who was giving the young surfer hell. The older man looked as fierce as always, with the huge, shark-bite scar on his side. "I'm taking him up to the clinic."

"Get back ASAP," Luis shouted back.

They hobbled off, Justin supporting Alec's weight on his shoulders. "So, where are we going?" Alec asked.

"Up to the clinic. Standard procedure for minor injuries."

"Minor, my butt. I can do the selfless-hero bit as well as you can."

They made their way across the sand to the boardwalk, exchanging insults all the way to the one-story clinic just off the boards. When they got inside, Justin lowered Alec into a chair.

"My man here has a boo-boo," Justin told the receptionist.

Alec offered Justin an obscene suggestion as Justin waved cheerfully and returned to the beach.

A few minutes later the door to the examination area opened and a girl in a wheelchair rolled out. She wore a long skirt, brown boots, and a low-cut red blouse. Alec took in the whole picture, bit by bit. The big rubber wheels on her chair. The slender body with just enough curves to make him forget about his ribs for a few seconds. The incredibly long, dark hair that cascaded in waves all the way down to her elbows. The smooth olive skin. The great eyes. He glanced for a split second at the chair again, then returned to her eyes. Big, round eyes, nearly black and fringed with huge lashes. The girl had killer eyes. The rest of her wasn't bad, either.

"Alec Wussy?" she called out.

"How about Alec Daniels?" he suggested.

"How *about* Alec Daniels?" she replied with a grin. "Your friend gave your name as Wussy."

"He would." Alec laughed, until he realized just how much laughing hurt.

"My name's Marta. Come on back." She turned her wheelchair neatly and propelled herself through the door. "In there." She pointed to one of the small examining rooms.

She followed him in. "Now, hop up on the

table. I need to take your temperature and blood pressure."

"How about if I just lean against it? I'm not hopping very well right at the moment."

"Me neither," Marta said.

For a heartbeat, Alec froze. Then he saw the laughter in her dark eyes. He relaxed and leaned against the table.

"Lift up your tongue," she instructed, shaking down a thermometer. She reached up to stick it under his tongue and closed his mouth with her hand. "Keep it shut."

Next she wound a Velcro strap around his right arm and pumped the little black rubber bulb that inflated the sphygmomanometer. She placed a stethoscope against his arm and listened as she let the air escape.

"Good blood pressure," she commented. "How old are you?"

"Eighteen."

"Keep your mouth closed. Eighteen. What a coincidence. Me too. Is there a lot of pain?"

"Hmmm," Alec answered.

She took his wrist in one hand, pressing the fingers of her free hand against the pulse, and watched the sweep hand on her watch. She shook her head. "Eighty-eight. That's kind of high. Of course, it might be lower if you weren't trying to look down the front of my blouse."

Alec jerked back, flustered and embarrassed. He hadn't been looking down her blouse. Exactly. "Hm-mm-mm hmming," he said.

"No big deal," Marta said. "I get to look at your chest. It's only fair."

Alec felt himself blushing, something he did not remember ever having done before.

"Oh, that's so cute," Marta observed mockingly. She gave him a lingering look, then pressed her hand gently against his side. "This the place?"

"Mmmm," Alec confirmed.

"Don't worry, I won't hurt you," she said. "I'll let the doctor do that." She took the thermometer out of his mouth. "Right on the number." She made a notation on his chart, then turned and began to move away. "Doctor will be right in."

"Thanks, Marta," Alec said.

She looked back over her shoulder at him. "I usually go out early in the morning to exercise along the boardwalk. Seven, seven-thirty."

Without waiting for a reply, she disappeared.

Grace twisted the knob until the water was almost too hot to bear, steaming her head and shoulders, cooling by the time it reached her toes. If she stayed in the shower a couple more days, she might just manage to regain consciousness.

Her head felt several sizes too big. This wouldn't take honors as her worst hangover in history, but it was definitely up there. The odd thing was, she hadn't drunk that much. A couple of beers before she'd gone in to work. The shooter she'd bummed off Anton halfway through her shift and her shift drink at the end of the night.

Oh, and the leftover martini of a customer who'd found it insufficiently dry. She'd forgotten that. And of course, she and Mike had split the last third of a bottle of Chardonnay a table hadn't finished.

Still, she hadn't *felt* drunk when she'd left work with David. So why did her head feel like it was going to explode?

Grace turned off the shower and stepped out onto the cold black-and-white-tile floor. One of these days, someone was going to have to spring for a bath mat. She pulled her bath towel off the hook on the back of the door. Something hanging alongside it fell to the floor. A jockstrap. Justin's, since he was the only other person to use this bathroom. She picked it up with a mixture of amusement and distaste and hung it back on the hook.

She'd just started to towel dry her hair—very gently, since the slightest movement made her feel like her brains were on spin cycle—

when she heard the phone ring in the hall.

"Can anybody get that?" she yelled. The throbbing in her head intensified, and instantly she regretted raising her voice. "No, of course not," she muttered. "They're probably all at work." Grace wrapped the towel around her and padded on wet feet into the hallway. She caught the phone on the fourth ring.

"Make it good," she said.

"Grace?"

Her mother. There was no mistaking the voice. "Yes, it's me, Mother."

"Grace, I need to know when you're coming to get the rest of your things."

Not one for small talk, her mother. But then, the time for pleasantries between them had long since passed. Grace leaned against the wall. "What's the hurry?"

"Norman is coming over tomorrow to go over some ideas with me."

Norman was a decorator friend of her mother's. Mrs. Caywood, who was a realtor, had sold him a condo two buildings away from her own.

"Ideas?" Grace repeated. She twisted a lock of wet hair and watched the drops land on the shiny hardwood floor.

"We're turning your room into a guest bedroom."

Her mother was removing the last traces of her presence. Grace was being permanently exiled. She'd known it was just a matter of time. What she hadn't expected was this icy knot in the pit of her stomach. Probably just the hangover.

Not that Grace wanted to return home. She'd left of her own free will and was glad, *ecstatic* to be away from her mother's mood swings, her drunken self-pity and drunker rages.

"I'll be there today," Grace said, her voice flat.

This time it was her mother who hesitated. *Didn't expect that, did you?* Grace thought grimly.

"Fine," Mrs. Caywood said. "I'll expect you after lunch."

"Expect me when I get there," Grace said. She hung up the phone and took several deep, calming breaths. Then she went into the kitchen and pulled a beer from the refrigerator. She twisted off the top and drank half the bottle before coming up for air.

It was a twenty-minute drive from the south end of town to the pricier north end, where twenty-story condo buildings replaced the ramshackle charm of Grace's new neighborhood. She parked her car in its old space.

Her father had bought her the little convertible as soon as Grace had obtained her learner's permit—less for Grace's benefit than to annoy his ex-wife. At least one good thing had come out of that divorce, Grace thought, patting the warm hood as she passed.

She stepped into the sterile coolness of the Sea Mist Condominium lobby. The walls were painted white; the art-deco-look furniture was black. The paintings were blandly tasteful. Grace punched the elevator button harder than she needed to. She hated this place.

"Grace, honey, where have you been hiding yourself?"

Grace turned to see Madeline, the elderly daytime concierge, waving from her marble desk.

"I moved out," Grace said. "To a house on the bay in the south end."

"The *south* end?" Madeline wrinkled her nose, but before she could say anything more, the elevator doors opened. Grace gave a little wave and beat a hasty retreat to the corner of the elevator.

To her mother, Madeline was just another condo perk, someone to feel superior to when she handed off her dry cleaning on the way to her job. Of course, it hadn't been enough for Ellen Caywood to buy an ocean-side condo with a concierge and an Olympic-size pool;

she'd had to have the penthouse with the wraparound view, too. Living well, Ellen liked to say, was the best revenge.

During the years that Grace's father had made it big in real estate, Ellen had slaved away as his secretary. While she'd typed up title searches late into the night, Mr. Caywood had carried on a none-too-subtle affair with one of his sales protégés, a girl in her twenties with a million-dollar smile and the sales to back it up. Eventually, of course, Ellen had wised up. Mr. Caywood had moved out to California, married his mistress, and started a new family. Ellen had made sure she got his share of the business in the divorce. Then she'd gotten her real-estate license and doubled the sales inside of a year. Whatever her faults, and there were plenty of them, Ellen was definitely a shrewd businesswoman.

Grace reached the fourteenth floor and stepped out into the hallway. The icy air-conditioning raised bumps on her bare legs. She had on her grungiest cutoffs and a T-shirt that read Property of O.C. Swim Team. It had belonged to Justin; Grace had swiped it from him their junior year. Of all Grace's boyfriends, Justin was the one her mother had most loved to hate, so Grace thought it most fitting to wear the shirt in her honor. Ellen had thought

Justin was a bad influence, a rebel, the kind of boy who would break Grace's heart. About those last two points, at least, Grace thought wryly, maybe she'd been on to something.

Grace walked slowly down the hall, girding herself for what was to come. She'd been away for only a couple of weeks, but already there was an eerie strangeness to being here, following the same path she'd walked every day for years. She stopped in front of the door. She still had the key, but this was all about *not* being a member of her mother's household anymore.

She knocked on the door and waited.

Her mother opened the door instantly, as if she'd been lying there in wait. She looked beautiful, as always—like Grace herself, with more years and a few fugitive lines here and there. Her hair was bleached to a cool blond, professionally set and sprayed. She wore a cream-colored linen suit set off by gold jewelry at her throat and wrists. Her eyes focused hard and sharp.

Good, at least she was sober.

"Aren't we formal?" Ellen said mockingly.

"Fair is fair," Grace said. "I don't want you walking into *my* house without knocking."

She strode into the well-furnished living room, with its black leather and chrome and its carefully tended plants. Copies of *House Beautiful* and *Vanity Fair* were fanned out on the glass coffee table. Only the ragged copy of *Skateboard* magazine betrayed the fact that Ellen didn't live alone.

Grace took a deep breath. There it was, that same familiar scent, part lemon-oil furniture polish, part Chanel No. 5, part stale scotch. She glanced out the window at the view she knew as well as her own reflection. On three sides, floor-to-ceiling glass opened on the ocean, the bay, and the long, narrow expanse of Ocean City. It was the only thing Grace liked about this place—the view of the world beyond it.

"Hey, Gracie," Bo cried. Her fifteen-year-old brother loped in from the kitchen. He was dressed in his trademark black—T-shirt, oversize shorts, and beat up Vans.

"Hi, Bo. What's up?"

Bo spread his hands. "I'm here to help you move your stuff out. You know, so Mom can turn your room into a guest bedroom." He rolled his eyes. "Like we have a lot of guests."

Ellen sent him a warning look, but Bo wasn't intimidated. "What are you going to do?" he demanded sarcastically. "Turn *my* room into the library?"

"Your sister chose to move out. If she's out, she's out all the way," Ellen said.

"Lucky her," Bo muttered.

"Come on, Bo," Grace said. "Let's go remove all traces of my existence."

"You're not taking any furniture with you," Ellen warned.

Grace shrugged. "I don't want any of it."

"You'll wish you had it when summer's over and you have to find another place to live. Have you thought about that? That house you're in is a summer rental." She strode over to a table in the hall and held up an envelope. "Georgetown University," she said. "They can hold open a space for you only another two weeks unless I pay the rest of the tuition money. They want to know what your plans are. So do I."

Grace dropped onto the couch. The leather was cold on the backs of her thighs. "Plans? Hmmm. Well, I'm still firming up my tanning schedule." She looked at Bo and smiled. "Between that and my flight lessons, I'm not sure I can fit college in."

"You're taking flying lessons? Awesome!" Bo leaped over the coffee table and straddled the arm of the couch. "Way to go, Gracie. When can you take me up?"

"You want to live to be sixteen, you better give me a while," Grace replied.

Ellen tore the envelope into neat little

strips and let them rain onto the coffee table. "A brilliant career move," she said disdainfully. "Maybe you can work your way up to flight attendant."

"Well, you have to start somewhere," Grace replied. "We can't all divorce our way to the top."

Grace saw her mother flinch and felt a familiar surge of power, followed by an equally familiar wave of regret. She shouldn't have said it, didn't even particularly *want* to say it, but her mother brought out her nasty side. It always happened. They'd fought like this ever since Grace was a kid, honing their battle skills till they both knew exactly which buttons to push.

Grace looked up at her mother warily. Ellen's cold green eyes bored into her, and suddenly Grace felt incredibly weary, unprepared to go the next round.

Was this how her father had felt near the end? Grace had never really been sure if he'd taken a mistress because of Ellen's drinking or if her mother had started drinking because he'd been leaving her, bit by bit, for years. Maybe there was no easy *because* for either of them. Maybe they'd just gotten tired, tired the way she felt right now, tired down to some deep, hidden part of her heart.

Ellen began scooping up the remnants of

the envelope. "So, I take it you're telling me that college is out?" she inquired without emotion.

"Why? Were you still planning to pay for it?"

"Not with that attitude, I'm not."

"That's what I thought," Grace said. "I guess I'll just figure it out myself."

"College, on what you make waiting tables?" Ellen scoffed. "I don't think so. And you can't get grants as long as I make what I make. You do know that, don't you? And while you managed to get accepted, barely, I very much doubt that with your school record, you'll be getting any scholarships. All those marks on your permanent record—tardy, unruly, disrespectful to teachers, absent without explanation."

Grace felt the barb sink in. It was true, all of it. Not that she was in any hurry to get to college, but still, she couldn't exactly wait tables at The Claw the rest of her life. She was too smart not to go to college eventually. But that didn't mean she had to have the whole rest of her life figured out by September, did it?

"Maybe Dad'll pay for it, Gracie," Bo suggested.

"Don't count on it." Ellen crossed her arms over her chest. "Your father has two other kids to think about now."

Grace considered a retort, something wonderfully cruel about her father's beautiful, fertile young wife, but she stopped herself. It would be too much effort.

"I'm having some coffee," Ellen said abruptly, spinning on her heel and heading for the kitchen.

Grace exchanged a knowing glance with Bo. Ellen preferred her caffeine with a touch of cognac.

They listened to her clatter in the cupboards. "You cannot just waste your life away, Grace," Ellen called from the kitchen. From a distance she sounded chastened, even a little conciliatory. Maybe she'd already taken a good swig of something eighty proof.

"You holding up okay?" Grace whispered to Bo.

"Yeah, no sweat," Bo said.

"You can always come stay with me again, you know."

"I know. But sleeping on your couch really sucks."

A slow creak in the dining room was the only clue that Ellen was raiding the liquor cabinet. Grace used to hate that sound. Now she just accepted it. Acceptance. That was one of the things you were supposed to do as the kid of a drunk.

Her father had forced Grace and Bo to go to a few Al-Anon meetings before the divorce, back when everyone was still trying to pretend they could put things together again. It had been one of those touchy-feely affairs in the basement of a church, a real weep fest for families of alcoholics, with lots of sobbing and hugging. It hadn't been a total waste, though. She'd met a cute guy there—platinum blond, tattoo on his neck—and they'd sneaked away during breaks to get stoned in the parking lot.

Ellen returned, mug in hand. "Did you hear what I said?"

Grace stood. It seemed to take every last ounce of strength she had. "I heard. But you know what? I'm too tired to plan my life right now. I'm sure I'll get my act together one of these days, and when I do, I'll drop you a line, okay?" She nodded toward what used to be her bedroom. "Come on, Bo."

They gathered up her belongings, which Ellen had already neatly boxed and labeled. When they passed back through the living room, Ellen was standing by the window, staring out at the gray waves, her mug clutched to her chest.

"You'll never be anything more than you are today," Ellen said.

It sounded like a curse.

Grace paused at the door. There was no point in answering, but she did, just as she always had. Just as she probably always would.

"As long as I'm not you," she said, "that will be enough."

eight

"Look, Chels, there's something I kind of wanted to talk to you about," Kate said late Monday night. Chelsea elbowed her aside, trying for a bigger piece of the bathroom mirror they were fighting over.

"What?" Chelsea asked suspiciously. "Does this have to do with me using one of the other bathrooms?"

"It's slightly more momentous than that. Actually, I'm thinking about getting birth control."

"Whoa." Chelsea's eyes went wide. "That is momentous."

Kate gave up the mirror battle and sat down on the edge of the claw-foot bathtub. "Well, it's not necessarily a commitment."

"More like just in case?"

"Exactly," Kate said, twirling a strand of hair around her finger. "Anyway, I called the clinic. I made an appointment for the middle of the day on Wednesday, on my lunch hour."

She looked hopefully at Chelsea. "I don't suppose you could make it, too, could you? You know, for moral support?"

"Are you kidding? I wouldn't miss it for the world," Chelsea said as she reached for the toothpaste. "You know I live vicariously through you, Kate. Maybe I'll videotape the whole thing for posterity."

"It's not too late for you to make an appointment, too, Chels."

"Me? What for?"

"You know . . . just in case."

"In case of what? You know I'm saving myself for marriage." She stared into the mirror as a horrifying thought grabbed hold of her. "But what if I never get married, Kate? What if I die an old, dried-up prune, never having experienced the magic, the ecstasy—"

"What if it's not all that ecstatic?" Kate interrupted. "Maybe you're right about waiting. I mean, I love Justin. I love him more than anything in the world. But still, you only have a first time once. It's like a bridge you cross over and then you can never cross back. Besides—" Her voice went soft. "I'm afraid it'll just make things harder if things don't work out with Justin, and—" Kate rubbed her eyes. "I don't know. The more I think about it, the more confused I get."

"Maybe you're thinking too much again."

Kate reached for a brush on the counter and began stroking it through her hair absent-mindedly. "How come you're waiting, Chels?"

"Well, to begin with, I don't even have a partner, Kate," Chelsea replied. "Weren't you paying attention during health class?"

"But you could have with Greg, for example. Is it because of your religion?"

"That's part of it, I guess," Chelsea said. "And part of it just feels like something inside me says to wait until I'll be with someone forever." She stuck out her tongue at her reflection in the mirror. "What a sappy romantic. I'm like something out of the Dark Ages."

"No, you're not. I really envy you." Kate sighed. "It must be nice to be so sure."

"Kate, it took me ten minutes to decide whether to have Rice Krispies or Grape-Nuts this morning. In the end it got so late, I had to settle for a rotten banana. You're the one with an opinion on everything."

"Except sex." Kate set down her brush and stood. "I mean, I don't even know *how* to have sex." She grinned slyly. "Well, okay, I think I've got a pretty good grasp of the fundamentals. But still. Remember when we used to practice kissing so we'd be ready if a boy ever tried to kiss one of us?"

"Sure. The famous three-step method—tilt to the right, slowly close your eyes, and pucker."

"My pillow and I spent a lot of romantic evenings together."

Chelsea nodded. "Yeah, but when that first kiss finally happened, it was, like, all over before I even had a chance to think about it. No tilt, no slow eye closing, no lip pucker. Just a blur followed by lots of embarrassment."

"I'm going downstairs for a Ben & Jerry's fix. Want some?"

Chelsea held up her toothbrush. "Too late."

"Please, Chels. Stop me before I eat again. It's Cherry Garcia. You know I have no self-control."

"That's why you're going to the clinic Wednesday."

Kate socked Chelsea on the arm. "One scoop," she vowed as she left. "Just one tiny little scoop . . ."

Chelsea brushed her teeth, washed her face, and did a quick zit check in the mirror. Then she headed down the hall to her bedroom. Alec's door was closed. He'd probably hit the sack early so he could nurse those bruised ribs.

Connor's door was open, though. She peeked inside. There was a yellow notepad on his neatly made bed, with a fountain pen next to it. Except for the stack of books on his night table, that was about it. She was really going to have to whip up a painting for his wall. The guy lived like a monk.

She went into her own room and flopped onto her bed. Enjoying the sensation, she continued to bounce up and down a few more times.

"Having fun?"

Chelsea jumped at the sound of Connor's voice. He was leaning against the doorjamb, arms crossed over his chest.

"Oh, uh, no. I mean, I guess yes." She grinned and stood up. "It's a new type of exercise. Bouncercise."

Connor took a step inside, and Chelsea felt suddenly self-conscious in her ratty pink bathrobe with the jelly-doughnut stain on the lapel. She glanced nervously at the lacy white bra slung over the back of her desk chair, at the open box of tampons on her dresser, at the pile of dirty clothes on her floor. Connor had probably been in plenty of other girls' rooms before, she reminded herself. The real question was, had he ever been in a slob's room before?

"I'm looking good," he commented approvingly on a sketch she'd done of him. It was on a spiral pad on the end of her bed. "Right there in bed with you."

"Coincidence," she said.

"Uh-huh." Connor grinned. "Sweet dreams." He gave a little wave and disappeared around the corner.

Chelsea closed the door and snapped off the light. Then she took off her robe and climbed into bed. The sheets were cool on her skin. The warm night breeze was sweet with the honeysuckle that grew in a wild tangle below her window.

Through the wall, she heard the sound of bedsprings depressing: Connor, climbing into his bed.

Chelsea wondered what he wore to bed. Probably, like her, nothing.

But then again, he was Irish. Maybe people in Ireland didn't do things like sleep naked. It was a chilly country, after all. And a rather strict one in many ways.

She'd seen him in a bathing suit, of course. He had nice long legs and a hard, flat stomach. A sprinkling of chest hair. Not much in the way of muscles, but then, if he kept working construction, that would change.

She wondered when he would kiss her. She had a feeling it would be different somehow—not because he was white, but because he was, well . . . Connor. Because he was smart, funny, mysterious, sexy Connor.

Once he had kissed her hands, a sweet gesture of thanks when she had discovered his secret and when she had promised to forget that he was in the country illegally. Of course, she could never really forget that. At any time, any day, the Immigration people could find him out and put him on a plane back to Ireland. At any time.

And then what?

Chelsea hoped he kissed her before that day came. And she hoped he didn't.

Maybe her life wasn't quite as simple as she liked to think.

The girl was floating in the water, just out of reach, a mysterious smile in her dark eyes, but if Alec was any judge of women, she was definitely interested. Of course, if the green scales where her legs should have been were any indication, she was also a mermaid, but who was he to quibble? She swam to him, pressed her mouth to his, kissed him, then placed her hand on his neck. "No pulse," she remarked. "That's so cute." He tried to explain that really, he was very much alive and interested in pursuing this, but his mouth seemed to be glued shut. "Hmm-mm-mm?" he asked, which, roughly translated, meant, *Are you free tomorrow?* But she was already swimming away. He tried to follow her, but his legs had turned to concrete. "See you at seven," she called as he was sucked down into the black, icy water. She swam by one last time, laughing as she passed, and gave a kick of her shimmering flippers, landing one hard in his ribs. Then she was gone.

It hurt like a mother, and Alec moaned, rubbing his side. He opened one eye. His clock radio was blaring some Madonna tune. He took a swipe, missed the off button, and sent the radio crashing to the floor. He cracked open his other eye. Sunlight streamed mercilessly through the venetian blinds. Slowly he rolled over and retrieved the clock. Six-thirty. Too damn early, but he was almost relieved to be awake. Man, what a dream he'd been having.

Gingerly Alec examined his ribs. There was an ugly bruise there, crimson with a touch of blue, about the size of a baseball. Okay, maybe a softball. He stood up carefully, shaking his head to clear away the sleep, and ran a hand through his blond hair.

In the mirror he caught a reflection of his body, painted with brilliant strips of sunlight peeking through the blinds. He flexed his shoulders. "Deltoid, trapezius, infraspinatus, teres minor and major," he muttered. He checked the far wall, where he'd hung four glossy posters showing the human circulatory, respiratory, skeletal, and muscular systems. If he was going to be a doctor someday, he figured he might as well start learning some of the basics.

He put on a pair of gym shorts and bent forward at the waist, grabbing his ankles to stretch. Good sign. It didn't hurt as much as he'd expected it to. Of course, it *was* only a bruise, as Justin had been careful to point out. Repeatedly. He dropped to the floor and did two sets of fifteen push-ups. Under the circumstances, he thought he'd skip the sit-ups today.

When he got to the bathroom, the shower was already going. The door was unlocked, so he opened it and got a puff of steam in the face.

Connor pulled back the shower curtain, his head lathered, his expression sour as it was every morning. "Oh, it's you." He closed the curtain again. "I'll be out in a minute."

"Don't rush. I don't need the shower yet. I'm going for a run."

Connor issued a snort of disgust.

Alec quickly brushed his teeth and splashed water in his face. There was a light knock at the door. "Who's there?"

"It's Kate."

"Who the hell?" Connor demanded, pulling back the shower curtain again.

"It's Kate," Alec said.

"Oh, then, by all means let her in. Why should I have any privacy while I'm taking a shower?"

Alec opened the door. Kate, wearing an oversize football jersey, was averting her eyes. "I'm dressed," Alec reassured her.

"I'm not," Connor said.

"I'm out of shaving cream," Kate said.

Alec laughed. "What do you need shaving cream for?"

"My legs, what do you think?"

"I didn't know girls used shaving cream on their legs," Alec said.

"I didn't used to until Chels and I snagged some of yours last week. It works better than soap."

"You can borrow mine," Connor yelled over the sound of the water. "Alec doesn't have any. The boy shaves only every six months or so."

Alec made a face, then gave Kate a wink. He pulled out a paper cup from the dispenser on the wall and filled it to the rim with cold water. Then he lifted the cup over the top of the shower curtain and spilled it.

Connor gave an outraged shout, and Alec

grabbed the can of shaving cream, handed it to Kate, and ducked out of the room.

Five minutes later he was on the street in blue gym shorts, a University of Texas T-shirt, and his well-worn Adidas. He did a couple more quick stretches. It was hotter than it should have been this morning, the sun hanging low and dull in a hazy sky, but dew still covered the grass in the front yard. The grass had been mowed, but the bushes were a mess. Maybe he'd tackle them later in the week. Bushes had been his assigned job at home. His big brother did the mowing; his little brother raked up. He trimmed bushes. The three Daniels boys, all working together on the yard. His dad's trick to get them all out of the house early on a Sunday morning so he could read his paper and watch *Meet the Press* undisturbed.

Alec started down the little street, waving to the middle-aged woman next door who was painting a picture of a seagull on her mailbox. When he reached the end of the street, he paused. Normally he ran along the bay front. The road was quiet in the early morning, and the recently resurfaced blacktop was perfectly smooth. He avoided running on the boardwalk because it was a little like being in a race; everyone was worried that someone else was passing them. As for running along the sand, that was way too much like what he did all day long at work.

But today he felt like giving the boards a try, for a change of pace. He was surprised to find the boardwalk quieter than he'd imagined. Just a handful of joggers were out, and only one doughnut shop and a sidewalk fast-food stand were open. Every other storefront was closed, protected by pull-down steel gratings and heavy locks. The sun was still low, alternately strengthening and weakening as scattered tendrils of gray cloud passed in front of it. This close to the water, the air smelled salty and rich. He loved that smell. It made him think about the summers he'd spent vacationing at the beach as a kid.

He wondered which way he should turn on the boardwalk. To the south, the boards ended in the silent rides, the Tilt-A-Whirl and Ferris wheel motionless, illuminated only intermittently by gold as the sun escaped a cloud. To the north was condo land. He'd have more open space if he headed that way, at least two miles till the boardwalk ended.

He turned left, heading north. Of course, he realized, the clinic was to the south. He assumed somehow that was the area where Marta would be. Better to keep going north, then. After all, if he ran into her, he'd have to talk to her, just to be polite. And he was here to run, to get a good workout, not to meet Marta.

He fell into an easy pace, not wanting to push his luck with his ribs. He passed a gray-haired man wheezing and fighting his way along, the headband around his balding head soaked in sweat. Up ahead were two girls. One, a blond with a ponytail that bounced happily as she ran, wore a sleeveless, white cotton top and black Lycra leggings that accentuated her firm glutes. The other was a redhead, her hair caught up under a green baseball cap, wearing loose, very short shorts that showed off perfect legs.

Maybe he'd misjudged the boardwalk after all. Alec slowly shortened the distance between them. The blond looked back, noticed him, and nudged her friend. The redhead ran a few more steps before attempting her own casual glance back at him.

He could pass them on the left or the right, closer to the blond or to the redhead, thereby indicating his preference. The girl he'd chosen would smile at him, he'd smile back, they'd exchange a few words about running and then name a place to meet later, a restaurant or club.

Alec had no doubt of that. Girls like this

always went for him. Always had. The pretty, well-toned, well-tanned, not-exactly-intellectual girls who wanted nothing more out of life than to be personal trainers or models or dancers in music videos. They looked at Alec and saw a kindred spirit.

It wasn't the worst curse a guy could bear, Alec thought dryly. You'd have a hard time convincing most guys that he was really suffering, being chased by beautiful hardbodies. Still, Alec knew, it was never the girls like Kate or Chelsea or Grace who went for him. They'd checked him out, sure, but then they'd just sighed and mentally set him aside as just another dull jock.

Alec picked up speed, gaining quickly now on the two girls. He passed on the left, carefully avoiding eye contact with either girl, and kept up his speed till he was well past them. He felt a moment of regret but didn't look back.

A few hundred feet away, the north end of the boardwalk was in sight. A run back would make four miles, which still was only a light workout. Another good reason to go back to his normal six miles along the bay.

Then a runner up ahead dodged around something. Alec caught a flash of something metallic and realized it was a wheelchair.

Marta, it had to be, heading toward him. Alec almost turned around. No. What if she saw him? He couldn't hurt her feelings.

He kept running, intending to pass her by and pretend not to notice her. But as he drew close, his eyes wandered, and his gaze locked on hers. Her hair was pulled back in a loose braid, and she had on a gauzy white skirt and a light blue halter top. She smiled, nodding slightly.

"Oh, hi," Alec said. "Aren't you the girl from the clinic?" He stopped his forward progress but kept jogging in place.

"Am I?" Marta asked.

"You remember me?" Alec began again, "I was—"

"I remember you, and you remember me, Alec Daniels, six foot one, one hundred and eighty pounds, blood pressure one-ten over seventy-eight."

Alec stared at her. "Wow, great memory."

"I remember what I want to remember," Marta said. "And you remembered I said I was out on the boards between seven and seven-thirty."

Alec shook his head, feeling suddenly panicky and confused. "I'm sorry, but actually I didn't remember . . . I mean, I come running here every morning."

Marta shook her head, still mocking him. "No, you don't."

"Sure, I do."

"No. You don't. I'd have seen you. You came here this morning because you wanted to run into me, only you figured I'd be farther south, by the clinic, so you ran this way because at the last minute you chickened out."

Alec stopped jogging in place. He hadn't really had those thoughts, had he?

"Well," he said, wiping his brow with the back of his arm, "I'd better get going."

"Go ahead," Marta offered.

"Okay."

Alec jogged to the end of the boardwalk and then turned around, jogging back at the same easy pace. He'd intended to wave good-bye to Marta and keep going. Instead he stopped beside her again.

"So you want to go out or what?" he demanded, feeling strangely annoyed.

"Are you asking me out?"

"Isn't that what you want?" he said in the same aggressive tone.

"Is it what *you* want?" Marta persisted patiently.

Alec shrugged. "I . . . where would we go?"

"How about dinner and a movie? I realize it's sort of traditional and all," Marta said, "but

I can pay my own way. I know you lifeguards don't exactly make a lot of money."

"Don't worry about that," Alec said, still trying to shake off his confusion. "I'll pick you up at seven tonight, okay?"

"I'm working late tonight. How about tomorrow?"

"Tomorrow, then."

"What kind of car do you have?" Marta asked.

"I have a Jeep," Alec said.

"I have a specially equipped van. I could pick you up. Otherwise I would need some help getting in and out of you." She smiled boldly. "You'd have to lift me in and out. But you're strong. Consider it exercise."

Alec nodded. "I'll pick you up. I mean, I'll come get you at your place. And I'll pay, too."

Marta told him her address and phone number. "I don't have any paper to write it down, but you're a smart guy. You'll remember."

Alec narrowed his eyes and looked at her. She returned his gaze unflinchingly. "What makes you think I'm smart?" Alec asked.

"Because I know enough not to judge other people by their appearances," Marta said softly.

Alec nodded. Then, with a wave, he turned and began jogging away. He had gone only half a dozen paces when he heard her call out, "But you do have a butt, too."

"Now, the important thing to remember is that if you climb too steeply, you're going to stall out," David said as his little Cessna circled out over the ocean. "It's just like driving a car—the steeper the hill, the more power you're going to need. And there's a point where you just don't have enough power available."

Grace gazed out the window and nodded, a gesture that made her swollen head throb. Below her, the world spun and dipped unreliably. She'd gotten pretty loaded at work last night. It had been Anton's birthday, and by closing time the booze had been flowing freely. It was as good an excuse as any, and after her encounter with her mother yesterday, any excuse was all it took.

"So," she said, trying to focus her attention on what David was saying, "how do I know when that's going to happen?"

"Well, there are formulas, and when we get closer to your written pilot's test, we'll worry more about that. But the practical answer is that you'll feel it." He winked at her. "Pull back on the yoke."

"Me?"

"Yes, you. You're the one who's learning to fly. I already know how."

Grace placed her hands firmly on the yoke. "Just pull back?"

"Just pull back."

Grace eased the yoke gently back, and the plane's nose began to rise a few degrees. She glanced at David for confirmation and pulled it farther still.

She could feel herself being forced back into the narrow seat by the increased centrifugal force. The plane pointed higher, bringing the clouds overhead into view. Instantly she noticed that the engine, which had been droning along steadily, seemed to be straining.

"Hear that?" David asked.

Grace nodded. "The engine."

"It's straining. If you climbed any more sharply, it wouldn't be able to keep up speed, there wouldn't be enough airflow over the wings, and you'd stall."

"What's that like?"

"Well, you ever ride a roller coaster? You know how momentum carries you up to the top, but just barely, so that you're almost motionless before gravity gets you and pulls you down faster and faster?"

Grace managed to smile. "That sounds like something to avoid."

"It's usually not fatal in a small plane. See, even if the engine dies, as you're falling, the wind turns the prop and starts the engine up again. Now, in a jet—" He looked away. "Well, it's a little more troublesome."

Grace pushed the yoke forward until the plane seemed to be flying level. She checked the instrument panel, just as David had taught her, to confirm the evidence of her senses. He'd said the instruments could be trusted more than her own eyes. This morning that was certainly true.

David patted her on the shoulder approvingly. "Good, you're learning. Now let's see if you can do the turn like I showed you."

Grace took a deep breath. It would have been a whole lot easier without the awful pounding in her head. Three aspirins had barely softened the sharpest edges of her hangover. And as the plane banked left, the spinning ground below made her stomach want to revolt.

Of course, she was in little danger of throwing up. She'd already done plenty of that early this morning. Now there was nothing in her stomach but black coffee and a beer. She'd always heard that a drink in the morning kept the symptoms of a hangover in check. And it had been all she'd been able to keep down.

With plenty of Scope as a chaser, she'd felt confident that David would never smell the alcohol on her breath. She certainly didn't want him thinking she made a habit of drinking beer in the morning.

The airport reappeared below them. "So, are you going to let me land?" Grace asked, forcing a smile.

"Sure," David said dryly. "Right after I parachute out."

"I bet I could do it," Grace said.

"Landing is the single hardest thing you do in a plane. Flying is easy. It's the ground that's hard."

David took over the controls and brought them in for a perfect landing. They taxied to the hangar and climbed out.

"Your first official lesson. And you haven't killed us yet," David teased.

Grace put her arm around his waist. "So is the lesson officially over?"

"As soon as our feet touch the ground, we're no longer teacher and student."

"Good," Grace whispered, "because I couldn't have waited any longer."

David pulled her close and kissed her gently. The pounding in her head seemed to grow more distant as he lingered over her mouth, then let his lips rain kisses down her neck, leaving her dizzy and breathless.

Suddenly Grace drew him close, burying her head against his chest and closing her eyes. "Stay here," she said softly.

For a long time she stood there, lost in his arms, warm, protected, safe. At last she reluctantly backed away. She was surprised to feel tears running down her face and quickly brushed them away with her hand. She had no idea why she was crying, not a clue.

"Is something wrong?" David asked.

"Wrong?" Grace repeated brightly. "No. I was just—" She paused. "Just feeling good being here with you."

"I'm glad," David said softly. He leaned close and kissed away a tear that had run down her cheek. And when she closed her eyes, spilling still more, he kissed those away, too.

"Can I see you tonight?" he asked.

Grace shook her head. "I have to work."

"Afterward?"

"Yes. Be there, David. Be there, okay?" She hadn't meant to sound pleading, but suddenly the thought of him waiting for her at the end of the night sounded so . . . necessary.

"I'll be there," David said, kissing her again, softly, gently, and burying her in his strong arms. "I'll be there."

nine

That afternoon Kate stayed late at work, helping Andrew and Shelby update some files. When she got home, she found the whole gang assembled in the kitchen. Alec was standing by the counter, staring blankly at a recipe card, Grace was browsing through the fridge, and Chelsea and Connor were sitting at the table, reading the newspaper. Justin was staring off into space, munching on an oatmeal cookie, his legs propped up on the table. Chelsea's CD player was playing, and in the laundry room the dryer hummed and rocked. Afternoon sun, warm and butter colored, spilled across the red Formica counters onto the floor.

Domestic harmony. Kate felt a sudden surge of unexpected happiness. She'd been feeling uncertain and a little anxious the past couple of days, but somehow this made her feel okay, this collection of friends and strangers and lovers in this great big old wonderful house. This was home now. *Her* home. It wouldn't last forever, even she and Justin might not last forever, but for now, for this summer, maybe it was enough.

"Honey, I'm home," Kate called. She walked over to the table and draped her arms around Justin. He looked up and gave her a kiss on the cheek.

"You missed," she said.

"Best two out of three?" Justin responded, pulling her into his lap and giving her a long, slow version on the mouth this time.

"Please, you two. I'm already nauseous." Grace slammed the fridge and ran a beer bottle over her pale cheeks.

"You okay, Grace?" Kate asked.

"Airsick, I'll bet," Alec teased.

"How was the flight lesson, anyway?" Kate asked as she combed her fingers through Justin's hair.

Grace brightened for a moment. "Great, really great. David's—" She shrugged, her green eyes falling on Justin for a moment. "Let's just say I can tell he's going to be teaching me a lot."

"You always were a quick study," Justin remarked.

Kate covered Justin's mouth with her hand

and rolled her eyes. Everyone bantered like that in the house, but somehow when it was Justin and Grace, she always had to remind herself that whatever was between them was over now.

"I'm making dinner tonight, Kate," Alec announced. "Vegetarian chili and salad."

"I'm impressed," Kate said. "And with your war wound, no less. Why are you so energetic?"

"Alec's in lust," Justin volunteered.

"Who is she?" Chelsea asked Justin.

"He's not saying," Justin said with a sly grin. "Very mysterious, this woman."

Alec wasn't taking the bait. "What's the difference between *diced* and *minced?*" he asked. "This recipe says I have to dice the onions and mince the garlic."

"I think minced is smaller than diced," Kate offered.

"Are you really up to this, Alec?" Chelsea asked doubtfully. "Last time I saw you try to cook, it was just oatmeal, and Connor had to help you out."

"I have to learn to cook eventually," Alec said. "Besides, I have a recipe." He waved the three-by-five card. "I got it at the supermarket. The checkout lady said it was easy. She said a monkey could figure it out."

"Someone run out and get a monkey," Connor said.

"How does this work?" Alec asked, holding up a small white bundle.

"It's garlic," Chelsea said.

"I know that," Alec said. "But how do you . . . how do you get it started?"

Connor rolled his eyes. "I'd better wash my hands. This looks like it's going to be a two-man operation."

"I hate to miss this culinary masterpiece," Grace said with a sigh, "but I've got to work tonight."

"Maybe you should call in sick, Grace," Kate suggested.

Grace laughed darkly. "Yeah. Sick and tired."

"Well, dinner should be in about an hour," Alec announced.

"Good," Justin said, dropping his head onto Kate's shoulder. "I think I'll go take a shower."

"Bad day at the office, dear?" Kate asked.

Justin shook his head. "Invasion of the chalk people."

Kate laughed. Chalk people were what the lifeguards called the very, very white tourists enjoying their first day in the sun.

"I broke up four serious fights," Justin complained, "one involving the use of sandals as a weapon. I also called paramedics twice for people with heatstroke, had to ask three women to put their tops back on, confiscated enough beer to fill a swimming pool, had to hassle about a hundred times with people playing their radios, and answered at least—at *least*—a million stupid questions. And that's not even getting into the rescues! You want to tell me why an eighty-four-year-old woman *who cannot swim* would take an air mattress a quarter mile out?"

Chelsea grinned at Kate. "Cranky, isn't he?"

"What he needs is a good back rub," Kate said.

"You offering?" Justin asked brightly.

"No. I just said that's what you need."

Grace took a swig of her beer. "Pay special attention to his neck, Kate. Justin can be a little stiff-necked sometimes."

"I thought you were going to work," Justin said pointedly.

Chelsea reached for the last of Justin's oatmeal cookies. "We should do this more often, guys."

"What?" Grace asked. "Aggravate each other?"

"No, *this.*" Chelsea swept her arm expansively. "Be all together in the same room. We could have, you know, house meetings."

"My family did that every Sunday," Alec said. "We'd discuss stuff. Sometimes my brothers and I would vote on important things."

"Just you and Wally and the Beav," Grace said, sighing. "Sometimes you scare me, you're so wholesome, Alec."

"Don't let my boyish good looks deceive you," Alec replied as he attempted to slice an onion.

"I think Chelsea and Alec are on to something," Kate as she gently rubbed Justin's shoulders. "We could debate the crucial issues of the day. Say, for example, who's responsible for the Gabrielle Rheese calendar in the laundry room."

"Hey, I just got that so Justin and I could keep track of our overtime," Alec protested.

Kate snorted. "Oh, that is really weak, Alec."

"That's all right, Kate," Chelsea said. "We'll get our *own* calendar."

"Who needs a calendar when you've got the winner of the O.C. Beach Body Hottie Contest right here under your own roof?" Alec asked, pausing long enough to flex his biceps.

"While we're airing complaints, who put that bloody wind chime out on the porch?" Connor demanded.

"*I* did," Chelsea cried. "Those are genuine brass cowbells."

"Well, they genuinely drove me stark-staring mad while I was trying to write last night," Connor said.

"See how we're all relating?" Kate asked. "Just like Alec's house."

"Pretty much," Alec agreed. "Except for the part at the end where my brothers and I beat the crap out of each other."

"Is someone at the back door?" Chelsea asked. "I thought I heard something."

Justin craned his neck to check. "That's just Mooch scratching at the screen door. It's Alpo time."

"I'll get him," Grace said. "I was just leaving, anyway."

A moment later Mooch came bounding in, his bandage frayed and dirty, his paws coated with mud. "He brought you a token of his esteem," Grace called from the hall.

"What is that awful stench?" Connor cried as the kitchen filled with a nauseating odor.

"I am outta here," Chelsea cried, leaping to her feet.

"Mooch," Justin commanded. "Come here, boy."

Mooch trotted over proudly, depositing something large, furry, and very dead at Justin's feet.

"Alec, you're on your own," Connor said, grabbing Chelsea's hand as they beat a hasty retreat.

Alec threw down his knife. "I can't cook with

that stink," he muttered. "I'm calling Pizza Hut."

"Number one on the speed dial," Kate instructed as she climbed off Justin's lap, carefully avoiding Mooch's gift. "Do I want to know what that is?" she asked.

"Was, you mean."

"See you at dinner."

"You're leaving me to deal with this? After the day I had?"

"Be sure it gets a proper burial," Kate instructed. She left Justin and Mooch and headed off down the hall, laughing to herself. Maybe this wasn't everyone's version of domestic harmony. It certainly wouldn't be her parents' version. All Kate knew was, these people made her happy. They were nice to come home to. And that was a pretty good start, wasn't it?

"By the way," Chelsea said that evening as she and Connor sauntered down the boardwalk, "this is my treat."

"I don't think so," Connor disagreed. "You're making even less money than I am. I know your parents are landed gentry, but you're making the minimum, so I won't have your charity."

"And since you're now rich, I will let you pay—half. Besides, we're just talking frozen yogurt, not filet mignon."

They paused at the edge of the boardwalk to watch the waves. "Did you see in the paper? There's a tropical storm out there somewhere," Chelsea said. "Look how big the waves are. They're beautiful, aren't they?" The white crests rose and fell hypnotically, glazed by moonlight.

Chelsea hesitated, letting silence fill the space between them. She wanted to find the perfect way to tell Connor what she was feeling. But the words seemed to get lost in her throat.

"Why is it we have such a hard time talking about . . . you know, about us?" she wondered aloud.

Connor stared out at the waves. "I don't know."

Chelsea paused. She felt Connor's arm slip gently around her waist. His touch reassured her, made her brave.

"I really like you, Connor," she said softly.

He smiled, nodding very slightly, his eyes still on the water. "I really like you, too."

"And I think you're . . . you know, sort of, you know . . ."

"Devilishly handsome? Rakish? Dashing?" Connor suggested.

"Attractive," Chelsea said.

"Attractive," Connor repeated. "Attractive."

"Very attractive," Chelsea amended, lowering her eyes.

"And I think you're beautiful," Connor said quietly. "Lovely. Entrancing. I haven't stopped thinking about you since that first day I met you."

"That's probably because the first time you met me, I was buck naked," Chelsea joked.

"You had on pants," Connor corrected. Then he smiled slyly. "But yes, that image was branded on my mind. And it does come back to me from time to time as I lie awake thinking of you in the next room. It's really very annoying. I'm not getting all the sleep I should. And it's not just those bloody cowbells."

Chelsea took a deep breath. The idea of Connor in the very next room, thinking of her while she thought of him—well, that was a dangerous train of thought.

"I think about you sometimes, too," Chelsea said quietly.

Connor pulled her closer to his side, close enough for her to feel the heat of his body and the rise and fall of his chest. "Wondering when I'll ever get up the nerve to kiss you?" he asked.

Chelsea laughed. "It's crossed my mind."

"How about now?"

"Now?"

"If we get past it, we'll be able to enjoy our frozen yogurt more."

"Come on, Connor. That's the best you can do?"

No, this is.

Connor reached for her with his other arm and turned her till she faced him. Then he drew her close till she was pressed against his chest, his arms wrapped low around her waist. She circled his neck and raised herself up on her toes. *Tilt, close eyes, and pucker,* some tiny part of her brain reminded her.

And then she didn't need any more reminders. Their lips met, soft and trembling. Her lips parted, and he kissed her deeply.

When they finally separated, it was only for a moment. This time Chelsea pulled him to her, her hands stroking his head. And this time she didn't close her eyes. She let herself see everything—the moon, the ocean, the whole world.

They pulled away reluctantly. Connor started to say something, but his voice failed him. Chelsea laughed. Then Connor laughed.

"That was so much better than I'd imagined," Connor whispered.

"Amazing."

"Shall we try it again?" he asked huskily.

Chelsea parted her lips and drew him down to her.

"Nigger lover."

Chelsea froze. Connor's eyes were wide

with shock. He let her go and spun around to see who had spoken. But all around them was a moving mass of tourists. There was no way to know who was responsible.

Chelsea felt something cold and horrifying well up inside her. A terrible feeling, part shock, part humiliation, part rage.

"Who the bloody hell said that?" Connor demanded of an indifferent crowd. Some people glanced his way, but most just hustled on.

"Whoever they are, they're gone," Chelsea said.

Connor clenched his fists and paced back and forth angrily. "Typical coward." Then he shouted it. "You're a bloody coward."

Chelsea took his arm, then instantly released it. "It won't do any good to make a scene, Connor," she said. "It's just the way things are. And you can't be getting involved in fights that might draw the police—and questions."

Connor stood motionless, his jaw clenched, the cords of his neck taut. He took Chelsea's hand. Unable to stop herself, she shied away.

He took her hand again, more forcefully this time. "It's just one fool, Chelsea," he soothed her.

"No, Connor." Chelsea shook her head. "It's not just one. It's a lot of them. Some black, too. If we . . . well, it won't be the last time. It makes people mad."

"Does it, now?" he snapped. "Good. So much the better."

"Connor, you don't have to do this. This isn't your fight," Chelsea said. *And it hasn't been mine, either,* she added to herself. Not in the well-to-do suburbs where the rich and near rich had learned to hide their hatreds a little better.

"Like hell, it isn't," Connor said. "Your enemies are mine, too. No one tells me who to care about." He pulled her to him. "No one tells me who I can kiss."

He kissed her again, gently this time, just grazing her lips. "Don't be afraid," he whispered.

"I'm not," she said. "I'm not," she said again, repeating the lie.

ten

"Well, our little lovebirds, out of the closet at last, huh?" Grace said sourly as Chelsea and Connor arrived back at the house.

"What are you talking about, Grace?" Chelsea asked. She was feeling weary. It had been a night of tremendous highs and shocking lows. A night that had never really recovered from two hateful words muttered by a faceless enemy. She and Connor had unsuccessfully tried to forget about it, walking and talking together for hours.

Grace looked up from the TV, which was swirling with the computerized graphics and logo of the local news channel. "The big secret romance. You two have been making goo-goo eyes at each other enough to make me sick."

Grace's voice didn't sound good-natured. It sounded sullen, even mean.

Then Chelsea saw the liquor bottle, wedged between the cushions of the couch right beside Grace. And the glass, held in a limp hand that lay across her lap. A quarter of the bottle was empty.

"I thought you had to work tonight," Chelsea said, changing the subject.

"David had to fly somewhere, couldn't make our date, so I called in sick," Grace muttered.

"What brand of sickness is it, then?" Connor asked.

Grace lifted the bottle and looked blearily at the label. "I have the Cuervo disease," she said, laughing at the joke. "The deadly tequila virus."

"Have you had anything to eat?" Connor asked. "If you're bent on a serious drunk, it's less painful the next day if you take some food and drink a little water on the side."

"Less painful," Grace repeated dully. Then she turned her unfocused gaze on Connor. "Should have bought Irish whiskey, shouldn't I? Old . . . Old whatever you call it."

"Old Bushmills."

"That's it. Very good." She pointed a finger at him. "You know, you could be a bartender. Even a waitress like me. Fine, fine career. Being a waitress."

"Let's go upstairs," Chelsea said, taking Connor's hand.

"Oh!" Grace slapped the side of her head.

"So Chelsea's finally gonna give it up?"

"Slow down, Grace," Connor said kindly. "You're already good and drunk. No point in getting sick, too."

Grace nodded. "Sorry. I'm being a bitch, aren't I?"

"No, we know you're just kidding around," Chelsea said.

"Chelsea's being diplomatic," Connor said. "You are being a bitch."

"Sorry," Grace repeated. She waved them off. "You two go on and have a good time."

Connor started toward the stairs, but Chelsea held back. There was something sad about seeing Grace just sitting there on the couch, drinking. She looked lonely. If only Justin were around, he'd probably know what to say to get her to go to sleep. "Hey, Grace," Chelsea said brightly, "do you happen to know where the boardwalk clinic is?" The instant the words were out of Chelsea's mouth, she regretted them, but it was the only thing she could think of to say to Grace right then.

Grace turned around and leered. "Well, well, you two *are* getting friendly, aren't you?"

"It's not for me," Chelsea blurted.

Grace's face grew sad for a moment; then she grinned lopsidedly. "Oh. Poor Connor.

Lucky Justin." She turned back toward the TV. "I can show you where the clinic is."

Great, Chelsea thought, shaking her head despairingly. Kate was going to kill her. That's just what she would want—Grace tagging along to the clinic tomorrow. Of course, Grace was pretty drunk. Maybe she'd forget by then.

Without another word, Chelsea walked upstairs. At the top, in the dark hallway, she sagged into Connor's arms. "What a night."

"That it was," Connor said. "It started better than it ended, eh?"

Chelsea smiled. "Maybe we can still turn it around." She stretched up on her toes and kissed Connor softly. He returned the kiss just as gently.

"Will you think of me when you're in your bed tonight?" Chelsea whispered.

"Nothing else," Connor promised.

Kate woke up with the dream still sharp in her memory. Juliana lying impossibly still on her bed, one hand reaching toward her nightstand and the nearly empty bottle of blue pills, as if she were pointing, saying, "See, this is how I did it."

Kate touched her pillow. It was wet with tears. She was used to it by now. She had this dream every now and then, usually when she was under a lot of stress.

She wondered why she'd woken up, then heard the timid knock on her bedroom door.

"Is that you, Chelsea?" she called out.

The door opened in answer. Chelsea was visible for a brief second in the pale glow from the hallway night-light before she slipped in.

"I hope I didn't wake you up," she said, sitting down beside Kate on her bed. "I couldn't sleep."

"That would explain why you were knocking on my door at . . . what time is it, anyway?"

"One-ish. I know it's late, but I had to tell you," Chelsea said, her voice oddly excited.

"Tell me what?"

"He did it. Tonight."

"He who? Did what?" Kate propped her pillow against her headboard and leaned back.

"Connor. He kissed me. We made out. We tonsil dived."

Kate smiled and grabbed Chelsea's hand. "Details, details!" This was just what she needed, a little girl talk, a little chatter.

"Well," Chelsea began. "First of all, it was great."

"Big, slow buildup, or did he just go for it right away?"

"It was pretty quick. He said I was beautiful—"

"That's always good."

"Also lovely and entrancing," Chelsea said.

"Entrancing?" Kate asked with a giggle. "I like that. It's not a word you hear very often."

"Well, he's Irish," Chelsea pointed out. "So then he seemed kind of shy—"

"Connor, shy?" Kate asked.

"Well, who wouldn't be around someone who is both lovely and entrancing?"

"Uh-huh."

"Anyway, we were going to get some frozen yogurt, so he—"

"Wait," Kate interrupted. "He tried the old, 'We'll be able to enjoy it more if we just get the big kiss out of the way.' "

"Exactly," Chelsea confirmed. "And naturally I fell for it."

"So, then . . . ," Kate prompted.

"Then comes the big kiss."

"How big?"

"Like it lasted for a week."

"Mmm-hmm. Tongue?"

"Of course tongue." She paused reflectively. "He's really much more gentle and sweet than you'd ever think."

"Anything else?"

"Kate, we were on the boardwalk in front of millions of people," Chelsea chided.

"So that's a no?"

"Very funny. We just kissed."

For a while they were both silent. Kate

waited for Chelsea to go on, but strangely, for Chelsea, she wasn't offering any more details.

"Um, can I ask you a question that's probably dumb?" Kate asked.

"Of course. Don't you always?"

"I was just thinking that, well, this is the first time you've ever kissed a white guy."

Chelsea fell silent again, and Kate was afraid she'd said something that had offended her friend. In the dark she couldn't read Chelsea's face.

"Someone . . . ," Chelsea began.

Kate heard a catch in her friend's voice.

"What, Chels?" she asked softly.

"Someone called Connor a nigger lover."

Kate felt her heart sink. It wasn't exactly a surprise. There had been kids at their school who'd had problems with the fact that Chelsea and she were best friends, as though they were each somehow being traitors to "their" people.

"Connor wanted to kill the guy, of course," Chelsea went on, "but whoever said it was out of there fast."

"Brave people like that usually are," Kate said.

"You know, the thing is, it won't just be white people," Chelsea said. "There are a lot of black people, too, who don't like seeing interracial couples."

"I hope most people don't feel that way," Kate said. "I don't think they do. Myself, I've always liked seeing black-and-white couples. It makes you think progress isn't impossible."

"Have you ever, you know, been attracted to a black guy?" Chelsea asked.

The question caught Kate off guard. She was tempted to lie and say no. But then Chelsea would think she was a hypocrite. "Well, one," Kate admitted.

"Who?"

"Oh, you already know," Kate said grouchily. When Chelsea just let the silence drag on, she added, "Okay, it's B. D."

"I know you've always had a crush on my brother, but that's different from thinking he's a guy you could actually be serious about," Chelsea said.

"I could be serious about B. D.," Kate admitted, adding hastily, "if Justin didn't exist."

Chelsea laughed, dispelling the gloom. "Ooh, can I tell him?"

"I'd have to hunt you down to the ends of the earth if you ever said anything to B. D.," Kate warned.

Chelsea got up to head for the door. "Can I at least tell him he's next in line if Justin—"

"Chelsea. I'm serious, now. Don't!"

"Okay. I'll keep my mouth shut, on one

condition," Chelsea said. "You have to not get upset about something."

"Upset? Why would I be upset?" Kate asked.

"Well, it's about the clinic. Remember you weren't sure where it was?"

"Uh-huh."

"Grace is going with us to show us the way."

By the time Kate found something to throw, Chelsea had disappeared.

eleven

"You know, Grace, you really could just tell me where the clinic is," Kate pointed out for about the tenth time. "I'm pretty sure Chelsea and I could find it by ourselves."

Grace gave Kate an ironic smile. "It's no problem, Kate. I enjoy helping out my housemates. After all, I am the local here in O.C., and I feel it's my duty to show you guys around."

"Right," Kate said dryly. She shot Chelsea a dirty look, one that said, *This is your fault! Why did you have to blab to Grace?*

"You shouldn't be embarrassed about this, Kate," Chelsea counseled. "We're all adults. Kind of. I mean, we pay rent. And my dad always says, 'Young lady, when you start paying the rent, *you* can make the rules.' "

"What makes you think I'm embarrassed?" Kate answered. "I think I'm being very responsible. That's not something to be embarrassed about."

"Absolutely right," Grace agreed. "You're dealing very responsibly and maturely with the fact that you've become a raging pit of barely suppressed lust and passion."

"I am not—," Kate began, but they were passing by a loud video arcade that drowned her words beneath an assault of beeps and bells.

Kate paused to glance up at the sky. The sun was hidden behind a heavy, menacing layer of clouds, the outer edge of tropical storm Barbara. According to the weatherman, it was supposed to blow away harmlessly over the next few days, but in the meantime Barbara was ruining the sunbathing, not to mention Kate's mood. She hated cloudy days. Or maybe it was just that she hated being tormented by Grace.

"You were saying?" Grace prompted as they passed the video arcade.

"Never mind," Kate grumbled.

At least Grace was sober this morning. She'd been drinking so much lately that Kate had begun to wonder if Grace had a problem. She and Chelsea had debated whether or not to say anything to Grace, but Grace wasn't exactly the kind of person who took kindly to prying. Not that she had any problem prying into *Kate's* personal life.

Kate and Chelsea had decided to take a wait-and-see attitude. If Grace needed help, in the end they knew she would have to come to that conclusion on her own.

They passed a french-fry stand where two guys, probably juniors or seniors in college, were munching out on a huge bucket of fries. They nudged each other and grinned as the girls walked by.

"They wanted me," Chelsea whispered.

Kate smiled. "How do you know it wasn't me or Grace they were flirting with?"

"Simple," Chelsea explained. "The two of you scare guys. One of you is too good-looking, and the other is too sexy. Me, I'm just the right amount of both. I'm much more approachable."

"I don't scare guys," Kate protested.

"I do," Grace admitted. "Wouldn't have it any other way." She paused at a little side street. "Turn here," she announced, leading them off the boardwalk. "It's that little white building."

"That's a clinic?" Chelsea asked doubtfully.

"Well, we do have a regular hospital in town," Grace explained, "but this is where most people come for what Kate's after."

"Thanks," Kate said, giving her a close-mouthed smile. "I think we can take it from here."

Grace shook her head. "Sorry. I have a prescription to refill while I'm here. Besides, I'm sure you'd like to have someone more experienced along."

"*Much* more experienced," Kate said.

Inside the clinic, a dozen people, most in bathing suits, were sitting in orange plastic chairs, browsing through tattered copies of *Good Housekeeping* and *Highlights for Children*. Kate went up to the small reception window. The middle-aged woman inside shoved a clipboard with a form at her. "What are you here for?"

"I'd like to see a doctor," Kate said.

"What about?"

"What about?" Kate echoed.

"Yes," the receptionist said in irritation. "You got sunstroke? You stub your toe? You having a heart attack? What?"

Kate felt a blush creeping up her neck. "It's kind of private." She jerked her head subtly toward the other people in the waiting room.

"Honey, just tell me. I don't have all day. You got the clap? Crabs? Herpes?"

"No!" Kate said in horror.

Grace leaned over her shoulder. "She's not that kind of girl, but she will be soon. She needs to see about birth control."

Naturally, she said the words *birth control* loudly enough so that the entire waiting room could hear. Kate considered slinking from the room in embarrassment, but she wasn't going to give Grace the satisfaction.

"Okay," the receptionist said. "Fill out the form and have a seat. When I call your name, you'll go in to see the prevention counselor. After that you'll see our gynecologist."

The form had the usual questions—name, address, social security number, and a checkoff list of diseases, none of which Kate had ever had. When she was done filling it out, the three girls found empty chairs and waited. None of the other people in the room seemed very interested that she had come for birth control. Possibly because most were busy with problems of their own—jellyfish stings, cuts, colds, sunburns, and at least one person who was certain she'd gotten food poisoning from a crab cake.

Others were there, Kate suspected, for the same reason she was. Were they all as embarrassed as she felt? Were they all as uncertain about what they were doing? It was easy to act cool about the whole thing, but what Kate was considering was pretty monumental in its own way.

Of course, she reminded herself, just because she got birth control didn't mean she had to use it. But it certainly did remove one excuse for not . . . for not doing it.

"Kate Quinn?"

Kate started when she heard her name and jumped up, still carrying her form. Chelsea and Grace stood as well.

"Look," Kate said, "I really think I can take it from here alone, all right?"

"No way," Chelsea said. "I want to hear what the counselor has to say. I didn't pay nearly enough attention during health class. But believe me, when you go in to see the doctor, you're on your own."

Kate sighed. Obviously there was no way Chelsea and Grace were going to let her deal with this in private.

They were shown back to a small office with a tiny desk and two cheap plastic chairs. Grace had to stand, wedged in between them. A moment later the door opened and a dark-haired, olive-skinned girl in a wheelchair entered the room.

"Hi. I'm Marta Salgado. Which one of you is Kate?"

Kate raised her hand. "Me." Her first thought was that Marta would have been quite pretty, if not . . . but then she angrily pushed aside the thought. Marta *was* pretty, chair or no chair.

Marta looked doubtfully at Chelsea and Grace. "Who are you two?"

"I'm here for moral support," Chelsea said.

"I'm not," Grace said.

Marta shrugged. "Well, I'd say this was strange, but I've been working here long enough that nothing seems strange to me anymore. What are you here for, Kate?"

"Um, I'm thinking about maybe getting some . . . you know. Birth control."

"Are you having sex?" Marta asked.

"No!" Kate said quickly.

"She's thinking about it," Chelsea interjected. "So am I, actually, but only in the abstract. Only if, say, Lenny Kravitz was planning to move to O.C. Or if I found out Denzel Washington liked younger women."

"Or if a certain Irish leprechaun came on to her," Grace suggested.

Chelsea rolled her eyes at Grace, then smiled. "He's always after me Lucky Charms," she explained.

"Thanks for that insight," Marta said dryly. "We have a psychiatrist here on Wednesdays and Fridays. He may be able to help you with those fantasies of yours." She glanced over Kate's information form. "Have you ever been on the pill or used any form of contraceptive before?"

"No," Kate said.

"Should you have?" Marta asked meaningfully.

"What?"

"She wants to know if you've ever done it," Grace explained. "I'm a little curious myself."

Kate kept her attention focused on Marta. "No."

"I thought so," Grace said with just the trace of a sneer.

"Hey, Grace," Chelsea said. "I'm a virgin, too."

"Please," Grace said, rolling her eyes dramatically. "I'm sitting here with the only two eighteen-year-old virgins in Ocean City."

"Actually," Marta said seriously, "it's not as rare as some people think. Not every young woman is having sex by age eighteen. A lot of people do still believe that sex belongs only in marriage. And a lot of others just want to wait until the time is right for them, or they're worried about disease." She favored Grace with a raised eyebrow. "And not that it's any of your business, but there aren't *two* eighteen-year-old virgins in this room, there are *three*."

"You're eighteen?" Kate blurted. "Isn't that kind of young to be a doctor?"

"Doctor!" Marta laughed. "Who do you think I am, Doogie Howser's sister? I'm just a volunteer here. I give you some basic info; then you go in to see the doctor. She'll do an examination and prescribe birth control."

Kate relaxed. "Oh. The receptionist said

you were a counselor, and I sort of assumed—"

"It doesn't take a doctor to explain what I'm going to go over," Marta said.

"And what is that, exactly?" Kate asked.

"We're just going to have a little talk. Mostly about condoms because whatever form of birth control you decide to use, you'll want to use them, too. Condoms are your best protection against venereal diseases and AIDS. Actually, only not having sex can totally protect you. But if you're going to have sex, you *have* to use a condom."

"Condoms. I know about them," Kate said confidently.

"Do you know how to put them on?"

"Excuse me?"

"Do you know how to put them on?" Marta repeated.

"That's not *my* job, is it? I mean, the guy . . ."

"Lesson number one," Marta said. "You can't assume the guy knows what he's doing."

"This one does," Grace interrupted sweetly.

That brought Marta up short. Kate felt the flush crawling up her neck again, but she stared straight ahead.

"Well, we always like to do a little demonstration. Just so you know," Marta said. "And there's no need to be embarrassed. We're all adults."

Chelsea nodded. "Yeah, we pay rent."

Marta opened her drawer and tossed a strip of square foil packages on the desk. "These," she said matter-of-factly, "are condoms."

Grace grinned knowingly at Kate. "Welcome to adulthood."

twelve

All day long at work, Alec had been unable to concentrate. He'd been uncharacteristically snappish to people asking questions on the beach.

He'd even been too distracted to laugh at one of Luis's dumb jokes. At lunch he'd declined to join Justin at Floaters and had wandered the boards instead.

Now, if anything, he was even crankier as he drove his Jeep along the main drag past a brightly lit Burger King, 7-Eleven, and gas stations. The weather was doing nothing to help dispel his bad mood. It had been overcast all day, and now there was no hint of the usual brilliant sunset, just an unrelenting gray sky. He told himself he'd gotten up on the wrong side of the bed. He told himself he was just feeling a little down. But down wasn't what he was feeling, and he knew it.

Trapped was more the word that came to mind.

He stopped at a light. A beautiful blond in a black Camaro pulled up next to him. She checked herself in her rearview mirror, then checked him out.

It was too late to back out of his date with Marta, wasn't it? Or was it? It's not like he'd never blown off a date in the past. But he'd never made a date with someone in a wheelchair before.

Alec knew this line of thinking was dangerous. Wheelchair or no wheelchair, Marta was no different, no more vulnerable than any other girl and shouldn't be treated any differently. But he just couldn't convince himself. He couldn't disappoint her. He wasn't that kind of jerk. He'd opened his very unreliable mouth and accidentally asked the girl out, and now he was going to have to go through with it.

The light changed, and the Camaro girl gave him a little beep before peeling out ahead of him.

Alec checked his watch. He wanted to be on time, but there was no point in getting to Marta's early. And when he did get there, she'd be nervous, so it would be up to him to be cool.

He *was* cool, too. Not at all nervous. Not at all.

Edgy, maybe, sure. A little . . . edgy, that

was it. He realized he was driving too fast and eased his foot off the accelerator.

Alec turned left toward the bay and parked outside the white brick, four-story apartment building. He checked his hair in the rearview mirror. He tossed an empty Coke can and some gum wrappers under the seat so the Jeep would look more or less presentable, then grabbed the bunch of flowers he'd bought on the way over.

Taking a deep breath, Alec headed down the wide sidewalk. When he got to the door of the ground-floor apartment, he knocked and stood waiting uncertainly, twirling the flowers in his hand. They were probably too much, too formal. Nobody did the flowers routine anymore. Still, he wanted this date to be special, for Marta's sake. They were even going to have dinner at The Claw. He would have preferred someplace else—someplace where, let's face it, he didn't know any of the help—but he'd told Marta on the phone last night she could have her pick of any of the best places in town.

The door opened, and he sucked in a deep breath.

"Daniels. What the hell are you doing here?"

"Luis?" Alec took a step back. "I must have the wrong . . . what are . . . I was, um . . ."

Luis looked at him, at the carefully pressed white oxford shirt, the gray cotton pants, the flowers. He curled a lip. "Those for me, Daniels?"

"Um, no, they're for . . . I must have the wrong apartment. I'm looking for this chick—"

"This *chick*? You're here at my house, looking for this *chick*?" Luis shook his head in disgust. "You know the name of this *chick*?"

"Marta," Alec said.

"She got a last name?" Luis demanded.

Alec shrugged. "I guess I never asked."

"Maybe it would be Salgado? Is that possible? Marta Consuela Salgado?"

A voice floated out from behind Luis. "Daddy, would you stop torturing Alec?"

"Daddy?" Alec repeated. "You're . . . oh." He closed his eyes. "Oh, man."

Luis nodded. "You *better* say, 'Oh, man.' "

He held open the door, and Alec saw Marta, wearing a long, formfitting black dress that fell almost to her ankles. Her dark hair was caught up in a French twist, and she was wearing large, gold hoop earrings. She looked beautiful.

She leaned over in her chair and pushed her father aside. Luis stood back but never took his gaze off Alec.

"Hi, Marta," Alec said weakly.

Marta grinned. "Hi, Alec."

"Now that we've all said hi, let me explain something," Luis said. He stepped up and put his face right in Alec's. He was a full six inches shorter, a fact that did little to comfort Alec.

"You're going to have my daughter, the apple of my eye, the center of my existence, the one person I care about, home by eleven," Luis announced. "Or I'll kill you."

"One A.M.," Marta said calmly.

"Midnight," Luis said, glaring at Alec, "or I'll kill you."

"One A.M.," Marta said, raising her voice slightly.

"One A.M.," Luis said. "One minute later—"

"I know," Alec said. "You'll kill me."

Suddenly Luis slapped Alec on the back, making him flinch. "I'm glad we understand each other. You're a good kid, Alec." He took the flowers from Alec's hand. "And thanks for the flowers. I love yellow roses. They remind me of Texas."

Marta rolled her wheelchair out the door. Alec followed close behind, not daring to look back at Luis.

"You know, you might have told me he was your father," Alec grumbled when they were halfway down the sidewalk.

"And miss the way your jaw dropped open

and all the blood drained out of your face? No way."

Marta rolled up to the passenger side of the Jeep. Alec had already gone over to the driver's side. "Oh," he said, when he saw her waiting there expectantly. "I forgot." He trotted around to her, then stood uncertainly.

"Just pick me up and set me on the seat," Marta instructed.

"Okay." Alec swallowed hard. It was a strangely intimate thing to be doing. He slid his hand around her shoulders, which brought his face close to hers. She smelled of some citrus-scented perfume. Then he worked his other hand under her legs. They felt thinner than the rest of her and didn't move in response to his touch. When he lifted her, he was surprised by how light she felt in his arms. He turned and set her with excruciating gentleness on the seat.

"I won't break, you know," Marta said.

"You won't even bruise," Alec answered as he folded up her chair, "or your father will have my butt."

"No, that's mine," Marta said with a smile.

Alec stowed the chair and climbed in. "Anything else you've been keeping secret from me?" he asked as he started the engine.

Marta made a back-and-forth gesture with

her hand. "I can't tell you everything all at once, can I?"

"Dry Beefeater martini up, gin and tonic, Chivas straight up, and a Bloody." Grace rattled off the order and set down her ticket so that Anton could verify the drinks and mark them off with a red pencil.

He began making the drinks as Grace assembled the garnishes—three green olives on a toothpick for the martini, a wedge of lime for the gin and tonic, a stick of celery and a lime wheel for the Bloody Mary. As Anton set the glasses on her tray, she quickly positioned the garnishes, then grabbed her ticket and headed away from the bar, making room for another waiter just behind her.

Instead of heading straight to her table, Grace detoured to the waiter station, a half-enclosed area where the coffee machines and electronic cash register were. She glanced over her shoulder, then pulled two small glasses from the pocket of her apron and filled them each with ice. Quickly she poured the martini into one, the scotch into the other.

It was a trick she had discovered early. When Anton made a martini "up," which meant without ice, he poured a slightly bigger drink. But Grace's customer had really wanted a different drink, one with ice. By transferring the drink to a glass with ice in it, Grace came up with a quarter shot or more of leftover alcohol.

She poured the leftover martini and scotch into her glass of soda. By this point in the night, the cola was almost half booze—gin, vodka, scotch—and she'd acquired a nice, pleasant buzz that made her feel relaxed and friendly. It was Grace's observation that she actually got better tips after she had a mild buzz. A little attitude adjustment. Besides, a Wednesday night wasn't going to get all that busy. She could deal with it.

She took a deep drink of her secret cocktail. If the other waiters even noticed what she was doing, which was unlikely given how harried everyone was, they weren't inclined to interfere.

Grace had learned that about restaurants. Several of the waiters smoked weed out by the Dumpster during breaks, at least one of the cooks never started a shift without two lines of coke, and most of the help worked the system to one degree or another to arrange drinks. Grace wasn't any different from them. She was just a little better at it.

"Grace, you just got a deuce on fourteen. This total stud with a gimp." It was Ann, one of the other women waiters, passing by on her way to the kitchen.

Deuce meant a party of two. Fourteen was the number of the table. The rest of the information was no more or less sensitive than that typically exchanged among waiters. Grace had said equally cruel things herself. When you had to be nice and pleasant to people's faces even when they were obnoxious, you sometimes compensated by being rude behind their backs.

Grace sighed and headed out to her station, looking across the room toward table fourteen. Sure enough, there was a girl in a wheelchair, parked facing the window. But when Grace got closer, she laughed. The "total stud" was Alec. By the time she'd reached the table, she'd recognized the girl as well. The girl from the clinic. Martha, something like that. Marta. That was it.

"Hey, Grace," Alec said.

"Good evening, sir, welcome to The Claw," Grace said. She suppressed a grin. Her "evening" had come out "ebening," but Alec didn't seem to notice.

Alec smiled. "You can cut the formality, Grace. It's just me."

"Certainly, sir," Grace replied with a bow that left her just the slightest bit unbalanced. "However, since you are going to be paying the same price as everyone else, and since you are obviously on a date, I thought you might enjoy our usual fine service."

"That doesn't involve you speaking French, does it?" Alec asked dubiously.

"Just my usual excellent service, for which you will reward me with an excellent twenty-percent tip," Grace said with a smile. She wanted to signal that a tip *would* be expected, friend or no friend. After all, she wasn't doing this for the fun of it.

"Um, Grace, this is Marta Salgado," Alec said stiffly. "Grace is one of my roommates."

"We've sort of met," Marta said.

"Nice to see you again," Grace said. "Now, let me tell you about our specials tonight."

She gave them the rundown—stuffed rock-fish, whole Maine lobster, and grilled mahimahi with pineapple salsa—and left them to think over their selections.

Alec and Marta. What's up with that?

Back at the waiter station, Grace saw Ann pause, stop suddenly, and utter a curse. "Butter. I forgot the butter again." She carefully set down a tray holding an appetizer order of steamed clams, a plate of caviar on toast points, and a glass of clear liquid. Ann beelined for the kitchen to retrieve the forgotten butter.

Grace looked at the tray. The clear liquid was undoubtedly vodka. People often drank chilled vodka with caviar.

She looked around guiltily. Ann was out of sight, and no one else was near, either. She would have to move quickly. Ann would immediately realize someone had stolen her drink, so Grace would have to be long gone.

In one swift move she raised the glass and tossed the vodka down her throat. It burned like liquid fire.

Grace slid the glass into the bus tray of dirty dishes and dashed away from the waiter station. When Ann discovered the drink was missing, she would have to go all the way back to the bar to replace it. But screw Ann. Ann was no great friend of Grace's.

By the time Grace arrived back at Alec and Marta's table, guilt was the furthest thing from her mind. Talk about attitude adjustment. Her attitude was way, way adjusted.

"So, so, so, you two," she said. "Made up your minds?"

"Um, I guess so," Alec said a little tentatively. "Marta's going to have the mahimahi."

"Oh, that's so cute," Grace said, eyeing Marta. "He's ordering for you."

"And I'm having the crab cakes."

Grace nodded. She felt herself sway and

leaned against the edge of the table to regain her balance. "Supersalad?" she demanded.

"What?" Alec asked.

"Supersalad. Do you want supersalad?"

"I think she means do you want soup or salad," Marta said, looking up at Grace with a critical eye.

"That's right, condom girl," Grace said, giggling just a little. "She's the condom girl, did you know that?" she asked Alec.

"Alec knows I work at the clinic," Marta said in what struck Grace as a snotty, superior voice.

"Does he know the other thing?" Grace demanded.

Marta's eyes flashed angrily, and Grace suddenly realized what she'd been about to reveal. A wave of embarrassment swept over her. Obviously the vodka was loosening her tongue. Her attitude had gotten *too* adjusted.

"Um, let me go and put your order in," she said, retreating so hastily that she bumped against another table, slopping part of an iced tea onto the tablecloth. "Oops. I'll come right back and clean that up," she called as she continued down the aisle.

Grace scrawled Alec and Marta's orders on their check. She'd never found out if they wanted soup or salad. Well, to hell with it. They'd get salads. Salads were good for you.

She burst through the swinging kitchen doors, narrowly missing Mike, the headwaiter. "You want to try walking with your eyes open, Grace?" Mike snapped.

She sagged against the counter, tore off the cover sheet of the ticket, and slapped it up in front of the cook. "Ordering," she yelled.

"About time, Grace," the cook said witheringly. "We've had an order up for you for about fifteen minutes. Where the hell have you been?"

"Hey, I'm here now," Grace growled, "so kiss off."

She grabbed one of the large trays and began loading on the platters of hot food. The plates themselves were hot as frying pans, but somehow the burning sensation on her fingers didn't really hurt.

She lifted the tray, slid her right hand under, and hoisted the tray up over her head. She'd held it for less than a second before it began to slip. She grappled desperately to control it but too slowly to avert disaster. The tray crashed to the greasy tile floor. Plates shattered and sent shrapnel skittering. Lumps of fish and slabs of meat lay weirdly out of place amid broken china and stray bits of escarole and dirt.

Grace covered her hand with her mouth. Then slowly, uncontrollably, she began to giggle.

"What the—" Mike was glaring at her, which only struck Grace as that much funnier.

Mike didn't see the humor. He grabbed Grace by the arm and yanked her over to a wall. "You're wasted," he snapped.

Suddenly Ann materialized, nodding and watching Grace through suspicious eyes. "I knew it had to be you," Ann said. She turned to Mike. "I had a vodka disappear from my tray."

"Hey," Grace said belligerently, "like neither of you drink?"

"I drink, Grace. I'm not a drunk," Mike said disgustedly. "You can't work. Get the hell out of here. Come see me when you sober up and I'll decide what to do with you. In the meantime you're off the schedule."

"Off the . . . I'm fired?" Grace demanded.

"I said come talk to me when you're sober," Mike reiterated.

"Screw you," Grace sneered. "You hypocrite."

Mike turned and walked away. Ann followed, shaking her head. Grace looked over at the cooks. They were averting their gazes, suddenly totally absorbed in their work.

"Hey, all of you can kiss off," Grace said, storming out the back door of the kitchen. Slipping on a broken piece of china, she fell forward onto her hands and knees. Grace picked herself up angrily, feeling the eyes on her, waiting for the laughter.

But no one laughed.

thirteen

Grace untied her apron and threw the wisp of black cotton into the air. It caught on the stiff breeze and skirted the shore before disappearing in a receding wave.

Come and see me when you sober up, Mike had said. The nerve of that hypocrite. Who was it who arranged so-called waiter meetings where they all did a shot at the bar when the manager wasn't looking? Who was it she'd seen out behind the Dumpster at the end of the night, passing a joint back and forth with his buddies?

Well, screw him. Waiter jobs were a dime a dozen in Ocean City. The Claw wasn't exactly the only restaurant in town.

Grace checked her watch. David had called that morning to say he was back in town and he'd meet her in front of The Claw at eleven. Looking forward to that had been half her motivation for going in to work that night. But it was only eight-thirty. At least it looked like eight-thirty. It was hard for her to focus on the hands of her watch.

Anyway, plenty of time to grab a drink or two. And she could use a drink after the night's debacle. She *deserved* a drink after listening to Mike's smug ranting. Not to mention Ann, who'd ratted on her for no reason at all.

There was a bottle of tequila back at the house under her nightstand, but if she went there now, Kate and Chelsea and all the rest of them would wonder what had happened. And Grace was in no mood to deal with their prying and good intentions.

Unfortunately, her fake ID—the driver's license she'd stolen from her cousin Vicky—was at home, too. She still had cash, though, the tips she'd earned plus the extra she carried in her purse. And where there was money, there was a way to get what you wanted.

Grace headed down the boardwalk, pausing every so often to catch her balance with the help of a bench or a trash barrel. She turned right when she reached Twelfth Street. There was a liquor store a block away. Glaring white light illuminated a tiny parking lot dotted with cigarette butts, squashed paper cups, and candy wrappers. Two men, dressed in ill-fitting, drab coats and baggy pants, sat in the dark alley next to the store, leaning against the wall. A paper bag, hiding all but the glass neck of a bottle, passed between them.

Grace went over to them, ignoring the powerful stench of urine as she approached. One man nudged the other, and both looked up at her expectantly.

"Got a dollar, lady? I haven't had nothin' to eat." The first man wore a stocking cap pulled low over cracked and ridged features. His two front teeth were missing. The second man said nothing, just raised the bottle high, shuddered slightly, and looked back down at the ground.

"I can do better than a dollar," Grace said. "How about ten?"

"Ten dollars?" The man licked his lips and climbed unsteadily to his feet.

"Yes. I need two pints of tequila." It wasn't a cost-conscious way to buy the booze, but a pint was easily hidden. "That'll cost about ten." Grace pulled a twenty from her purse. "You keep the change."

The man looked craftily at the twenty, the gears in his brain almost visibly turning.

"Don't even think about cheating me," Grace warned. "I may want your services again someday. You'll make out better by playing it straight."

The man nodded, apparently accepting her

reasoning. He snatched the twenty and disappeared inside the bright haze of the store. Grace tapped her foot impatiently, waiting for him to return. Finally the door opened and the man emerged.

He handed Grace a paper bag containing two small bottles. In his other hand he carried a bottle of cheap fortified wine.

"Share a snort with us?" the old man offered.

"No," Grace said, recoiling.

The man gave a hard laugh, revealing more of his rotted, neglected teeth. "Too good, huh? Too good to share a snort with a couple of old winos?"

"It's not that," Grace said.

"Oh, sure it is. You think you're different, too good, too hoity-toity." He stepped closer, assaulting Grace with his breath and the stench of his body. "But you're like us. You'll be back."

Grace turned on her heel and headed back toward the beach, the man's words ringing in her ears. Stupid old man. Not everyone who enjoyed a drink ended up a wino in a dark alley. Not everyone who liked an occasional buzz was an alcoholic.

She climbed to the boardwalk and pushed her way through the milling throngs onto the dark sanctuary of the beach. Out beyond the lights she could sit down and relax. Have a drink and get a grip on what had turned into a very, very bad day.

Halfway across the sand she reached in and pulled out one of the bottles. She twisted off the plastic cap and put the mouth of the bottle to her own. The liquid was sweet and burned going down.

"Better. Much better," she said, sinking down to the sand with a sigh. She took another drink. "Good-bye to Mike and The Claw," she said, raising the bottle to the moon, just a dull glow behind the clouds. "Here's to never waiting tables again."

Clumsily Grace turned herself around so she could face the boardwalk. She wanted to see David when he got there. As she tried to sit up straight, she fell over. She didn't care. It was hysterically funny, actually, and besides, it felt good to lie sideways on the cold sand, letting the lights of the boardwalk blur and meld and dance.

"I guess it's too late for a movie," Alec said as he pushed Marta's wheelchair out onto the boardwalk. "Dinner took longer than I thought it would."

"It was great, though, wasn't it?" Marta asked, looking up at him.

"Great," Alec repeated, smiling at her. "Food wasn't bad, either."

They kept moving along the boardwalk at a nice, slow pace. The moon was blotted by clouds, making the garish neon of the amusement park at the south end seem unnaturally bright. The waves were still high. Loud, too, as they crashed with more violence than usual on the empty beach. A strong breeze, oddly warm, grabbed at Marta's hair and blew long, stray tendrils back, teasing Alec's hands as he gripped the handles of her wheelchair.

It amazed him how relaxed he'd felt with her at dinner, relaxed enough to tell corny family stories and bad jokes, relaxed enough to actually feel comfortable just being himself. Marta was able to make him believe just about anything was possible. When he'd talked about his dreams of going to med school and his fears that he might not make the grade, she'd just shrugged and said matter-of-factly, "Of *course* you'll make it if you really want to." She had this wonderful, take-on-the-world energy about her that made him forget the wheelchair, forget everything except that incandescent smile and those huge, smoldering eyes.

But out here on the boardwalk, it was impossible to forget her wheelchair. The occasional stares and whispers made it impossible. The wheels, catching on the uneven boards and fighting Alec every step, were a constant reminder.

And this uneasy feeling in his gut made it difficult, too. He wasn't sure where to take this whole thing now. With other girls, sure, he had the moves down to an art. But Marta wasn't like other girls.

"I wonder what happened to Grace?" Alec asked. "I know the waiter who took over for her said she was sick, but it was an awfully sudden illness."

"She was drunk," Marta said flatly. "Faced. Couldn't you tell?"

"Yeah, I kind of could, I guess."

"Does she have a drinking problem?"

Alec considered. "I don't know. Grace likes to drink beer, but so do a lot of people. I've never seen her drunk before, though."

They neared a bicycle- and moped-rental stand, and Alec eased Marta's wheelchair to the other side of the boardwalk to avoid passing directly in front of it. It was idiotic, of course. She'd probably passed this stand a thousand times herself. But the reminder of what she couldn't do made him feel uncomfortable and protective all at once.

He felt the smooth warmth of Marta's

hand on his forearm. "Look," she said, "if we can't make a movie, I have another idea."

"Fire away."

"Let's go to your Jeep. I know a great place we can drive to."

"Good idea." He was relieved to have a destination, any destination, at last.

Alec turned her wheelchair around and headed back toward the ramp that led to the street. As before, he lifted Marta gently into the Jeep, folded up the chair, and climbed in beside her.

He gunned the Jeep and pulled down the street, heading toward the causeway that joined Ocean City to the mainland. As they picked up speed, Alec glanced over at Marta. She'd let down her braid, and her long hair streamed out behind on the wind. She was smiling to herself, eyes closed, hands clasped behind her neck.

"You can ask it now, Alec," she said, her eyes still closed.

"Ask what?"

"It. The question you carefully avoided all through dinner."

Alec squirmed uncomfortably in his seat and tightened his grip on the steering wheel. The rough, patched surface of the bridge rumbled beneath the Jeep's oversize tires. "Since you seem to think you can read my mind, why don't you tell me what the question is?" he demanded grumpily.

"Actually, you have two questions. I'll answer the first one. I got shot. We lived in Los Angeles in those days, me and my dad. My mom, too, then, before she bailed out on us. I was in sixth grade, walking up the front steps of my school, when two guys from rival gangs decided to stage a little shoot-out. They weren't very good shots and didn't hit each other. Instead they killed one girl and crippled another. Me."

Alec clutched at the wheel wordlessly, his eyes locked on the road. It was worse than all the things he'd imagined. There was nothing he could say, and he knew it.

"My dad decided after I got out of the hospital that we'd seen enough of L.A. He moved us here—as far from L.A. as we could get." She paused. "Something good came of it, anyway. O.C. beats L.A."

"Sixth grade," Alec repeated softly. "You were just a kid."

"Yeah. Turn right as soon as you get off the causeway. It's a little dirt road, so pay attention."

"Where are we going?"

"A place that only the locals know about. It's kind of a secret."

"Well, I'm not a local. Are you sure you're not violating some sacred trust?"

"There, there, turn!"

Alec slammed on his brakes and pulled the Jeep sharply to the right, slowing still further to negotiate the potholes and bumps of a pitch-black dirt road. Within seconds the lights of the bridge were gone, and all he could see was twenty feet at a time of twisting dirt road, closely hemmed in by shrubs and squat pine trees.

A sudden bump made Alec flinch. "Great idea, Marta. Now I'm going to bust an axle and we'll have to walk out of here." Instantly he realized what he'd said. "Damn. Sorry."

"Because you said the word *walk?*" Marta snapped. "Look, Alec, if you and I are going to be friends, we have to get one thing straight. I don't burst into tears when someone talks about walking or running or ballet dancing. I don't do the pity thing, all right? Period. So don't dance around, and don't walk on eggshells, and don't treat me like I'm made of porcelain."

"Sorry," Alec said as he fought the wheel of the Jeep.

"And don't apologize. I had a bit of bad luck, which happens sometimes. I handled it. Which only means that I've been tested, and I passed the test."

"Great, so you're the toughest person on wheels," Alec said in exasperation. "Are you going to tell me now where we're headed?"

"Right here. Stop. Turn off your engine, and kill the lights."

"Are you sure?"

"Yes."

Alec did as she instructed. Sudden darkness and silence fell over them. After a few moments the moon made a brief, hopeful appearance, peering shyly over a bank of black clouds, and Alec caught sight of a silvery glimmer of light just beyond the trees to his right. Gradually the silence turned out to be full of sounds, subtle and soothing. The breeze rustling the trees, the steady, strong lapping of the water, the noisy musings of some crickets.

"Come on," Marta said, her voice lowered to a whisper.

"Come on where?"

"I need you to carry me."

Alec climbed out of the Jeep and made his way around to her side. He had almost gotten used to lifting her up, used to the feel of her withered legs and the sensation of her weight in his arms. The one thing he had not gotten used to was the nearness of her face as he carried her. The way her eyes looked huge and luminous, the scent of her perfume, the rise and fall of her breasts.

"There," Marta said, pointing with her chin.

Alec carried her through a line of low bushes, ducking under tree branches he could barely see. Packed pine needles crunched beneath his shoes. Suddenly he realized he was walking on sand. The trees were all behind them, and they were on a tiny, perfect beach, curved as a quarter moon. It was hidden from the dirt road by trees, and absolutely private.

The dark water slapped against the sand, urged on by the strong breeze. Across the bay were the glittering lights of Ocean City.

"This is beautiful," Alec said.

"Yes, it is," Marta agreed. "You can put me down now."

"What if I don't want to?"

Marta smiled and nuzzled her forehead against his neck, sending shivers running the length of his spine. "Let's go in for a swim," she said. "The bay's always warm."

"Swim? I don't have a bathing suit," Alec pointed out. But what he was really wondering was whether or not Marta *could* swim.

"I have mine on under my dress. You can just wear your underwear. Come on," Marta said. He could feel the heat of her breath as her lips just grazed his neck. "Listen, sooner or later you're going to have to see what the rest of me looks like. If it's going to scare you off, well . . . look, I like you, Alec. I don't want to like you any more than I already do if you're just going to take off."

It was the closest Marta had been to uncertainty, the only brief moment of vulnerability Alec had seen in her. He pulled her closer.

But even as he held her in his arms, he was uncertain. The idea of seeing Marta in a bathing suit made him nervous. What if he couldn't handle it? What if it showed on his face?

Slowly he knelt and set Marta down on the sand. She used her hands to hold herself upright. "You'll have to help me," she said. "If I use my hands, I'll fall over. Just unzip the back of my dress."

Alec realized his gulp of surprise was audible.

Marta laughed. "Oh, come on, Alec. I doubt if it's your first girl's zipper."

Alec swallowed hard again and began fumbling for the zipper. His fingers were trembling as he undid the back of her dress.

He pulled off his pants and shirt while Marta shrugged off the dress, revealing a low-cut, white, one-piece bathing suit. "Now," she said, her eyes locked on his, "just lift me up."

He did, sliding his hand again beneath her legs, this time touching flesh, not fabric.

"This is what I look like," Marta said solemnly.

Alec met her gaze, then let his eyes travel the length of her body.

It was as if someone had joined two very different people. He saw a woman with strong shoulders, hard but shapely arms built up by years of moving her wheelchair, full breasts, flat stomach . . . and then, attached to her body, a little girl, with spindly, knobby-kneed legs and bony feet that didn't quite point the right way.

Alec heard Marta hold her breath, waiting for his next words. He wanted to say just the right thing, the sensitive, caring thing, but everything that kept coming to mind seemed so inane.

He shrugged. "I've never been much of a leg man, myself."

Marta's sudden explosion of laughter seemed to light up the night. "You're all right, Alec Daniels," she said affectionately. "Let's go in."

Alec carried her into the water until it was waist level, then he lowered her in. She immediately propelled herself away from shore, out into deeper water. Alec followed.

"Now we're on more equal terms," she said,

giggling as he trod water beside her. "This seems like a good time to answer that second question you've been too polite to ask me."

"There wasn't any second question," Alec lied.

"You're such a lame liar," Marta said mockingly. "You know my legs don't work. You want to know if everything else does."

It was Alec's turn to laugh. "It may have crossed my mind."

Marta smiled. "I'm flattered it did."

"So what's the answer?"

"The answer is, I'm pretty sure it does. But neither of us is going to find out tonight." She splashed him in the face with a handful of water.

Alec swam to her and caught her around the waist. "I have one other question."

"What?" she asked.

"Are you going to kiss me or what?"

"That's a question I can answer right now," Marta said.

Alec pulled her to him, holding her up in the water with kicks from his powerful legs, and kissed her as if it was the first kiss he'd ever known.

Grace woke with a start. Something had bitten her sharply on the leg. She slapped at the spot. Then, in a sudden panic, she looked at her watch, twisting the dial to read it in the faint light. Eleven-fifteen!

She lurched to her feet, feeling sick and woozy. Sand stuck to her face, and she tried unsuccessfully to brush it off. Her left arm was buzzing with pins and needles as blood rushed back into it.

There, on the boardwalk, in front of The Claw, she could make out the figure of a man standing patiently, hands in the pockets of his leather jacket.

Grace began running toward the light. She stumbled and fell on her face but climbed up again. "David!" she shouted.

David turned toward the sound of her voice, staring uncertainly into the dark. Then he waved as she emerged from the gloom.

"Grace! I thought you'd be coming out of the restaurant. What are you doing out on the beach? Get off work early?"

He smiled. She'd never seen anything as wonderful as that smile. She ran the last few steps to him and threw her arms around him wildly, nearly knocking him off balance. "Glad I didn't miss you, David, beautiful David," she gushed. She tried to kiss him, but he held her away, staring. It was as if a light had gone out in his eyes. His expression turned hard.

"Grace, you're drunk."

"Not very drunk, just drunk enough, if you know what I mean." She winked and gave him what she hoped was a sexy look.

"Grace, I know drunk, believe me. You're in bad shape."

Sudden anger exploded inside Grace, instantly wiping away all the warm feelings. "Hey, I don't need your crap, all right? I've had enough of that holier-than-thou routine for one night."

"You got fired, didn't you?" David said softly.

Even in her anger, Grace was taken aback. How could David know that? "No," she answered. "I quit. I quit that stinking dump."

"How long have you been drinking?" David asked.

"What?"

"I asked how long have you been drinking. You're only eighteen; when did you start? A year ago? Two?"

"What business of yours is it?" Grace demanded.

"You drink every day, don't you? Every night. Not always till you're drunk, but enough," David said. It wasn't a question. It was a flat statement. "You sneak drinks and drink alone in your room. And you drink to get over hangovers."

"You know what?" Grace pointed a playful

finger at David. "What *you* need is a drink, that's what I think. Loosen you up a little. You know, you can take me home right now."

David's mouth was set in a grim line. "I'll drive you to your house."

"My . . . no, no, no, I want to do it at your house. Have a couple more shots, put on some nice music . . . I'll bet you're good, aren't you? I know I'm good." She grabbed for him, tried to slip her hands inside his jacket, but he took a step back.

"Grace, go home," David said coldly. "Sleep it off and tomorrow get some help."

Grace eased close again, wrapping her leg around the back of his and pressing close. "I need some help right now."

David pushed her away. "Alcoholics Anonymous meets on Saturday evening in a room behind city hall, Grace."

Again rage boiled up inside her. She pounded her fists against his chest. "Leave me alone, you bastard. Get out of here. Go away, go away." She pushed him, and David moved back. Suddenly the distance between them seemed immense.

"I'll see you, Grace."

David turned on his heel and walked away, leaving Grace to stand alone on the boardwalk, clutching a cool, hard bottle to her chest.

fourteen

Kate slipped out of her clothes the next evening, letting her shorts and shirt join her socks and shoes in a pile on the floor. She'd spent the day helping Shelby dissect a shark that had washed up on the beach. Since it had been tagged by Safe Seas, the carcass had been brought to the foundation to be examined.

It hadn't been a fun day. Kate was pretty sure her clothing would have to be burned. There was no other way to remove that awful smell.

She was on her way into the shower when she glanced out the window. The bay was dark with low-slung clouds and there wouldn't be a visible sunset, but it had been days since she'd had any real exercise. She could feel the bunched tension in her shoulders and neck.

She slipped into a one-piece bathing suit, a blue Speedo she used for real workouts. As an afterthought, she grabbed a bottle of natural liquid soap and headed downstairs on bare feet.

Chelsea was flopped in the La-Z-Boy, watching *Oprah*. Grace was crashed out on one of the couches, sleeping fitfully.

"Grace must have had a tough night," Kate commented.

Chelsea shrugged. "I don't know. I found her this way when I got home from work. I hope she doesn't have to go to work tonight." She lowered her voice. "Do you think we should—you know—talk to her?"

Kate sighed. "What could we tell Grace that she would possibly care to hear? You know what everyone says—she has to *want* help."

Suddenly an image of her sister came to her, of Juliana slowly, inexorably fading from her family's grasp, growing more distant until they'd lost her altogether. Maybe it was true that they couldn't really help Grace. But she was their friend. They had to try, didn't they?

"Look," Kate said in a hushed voice. "Let's talk to her together. Some morning, maybe, when her head's clear." She shrugged. "It probably won't do any good, but still."

"Good idea," Chelsea agreed.

"I'm going for a swim."

Chelsea tilted her head and looked at Kate speculatively, then shook her head. "No, you don't *look* any different."

"What are you talking about?"

Chelsea grinned slyly. "You know. You don't have that special *womanly* glow."

Kate sighed. "Look, just because I happen to have a purse full of condoms and I started on the pill, that doesn't mean I have to run right out and . . . and acquire a womanly glow."

She calmly stuck out her tongue at Chelsea, then turned and headed out the door. She broke into a run across the lawn and out onto the pier. When she reached the end, she tossed her soap aside and executed a nice dive. Water closed over her, warm and comforting. Then she broke the surface and sucked in air.

For the next half hour she swam far out into the bay, keeping a careful eye out for the occasional Jet Ski or motorboat. Fortunately, the gloomy weather had cut way down on waterborne traffic. If tropical storm Barbara didn't drag her skirts away from the coastline soon, businesses throughout the town would start to suffer.

After a while Kate wandered back to the pier and snagged the bottle of soap. She lathered her hair and dove deep to rinse it, enjoying the way her hair swirled around like a slow-motion tornado. She twisted and turned underwater, relishing the eerie silence.

Then, between a pair of pilings, she saw a flash of silver on the sandy bottom. She swam farther until she realized the hull of Justin's boat was right in front of her, like a blue-and-white wall that reached nearly to the bottom. With the last of her breath she grabbed the silvery object and loosened it from the sand. It was a hammer.

Kate shot to the surface and came up inside the boathouse, in the narrow space between the boat and the catwalk. She slipped the hammer onto the catwalk for Justin to find, like some mysterious gift from the sea. It was undoubtedly his, anyway.

Then she heard music coming from the loft. An old Motown song, "When a Man Loves a Woman," playing on Justin's radio. Justin was near his bed, humming along. As a matter of fact, she realized in surprise, he was dancing along, although calling it "dancing" might be stretching the point. "Bouncing" was more like it.

When a man loves a woman, can't keep his mind on nothin' else. . . . Suddenly Justin executed a nice little pirouette, and his dance partner came into view, all sixty-five furry pounds of him. Mooch stood on his hind legs, tail wagging at warp speed, his big paws splayed on Justin's bare chest, his head bandage at a jaunty angle like a bad toupee.

Justin did a slick dip, and Mooch responded with a fervent tongue kiss to the chin. It was silly and touching and sweet all at the same time; Kate didn't know whether to laugh or cry. Instead she ducked beneath the water before Justin could see her.

She slipped through the pilings again and came up by the pier. She'd just hoisted herself up onto the boards when she noticed Justin standing there looking down at her, one eyebrow arched suspiciously. Mooch sat by his side. It was pretty obvious they were on to her.

"Well, if it isn't Fred and Ginger," Kate said.

Justin helped her to her feet, still frowning.

"I'm sorry, really I am," she added. "I didn't know you were home."

"Yeah, right." Justin tried to maintain the frown, but one tiny corner of his mouth betrayed the start of a smile. "We were having a private moment, Kate."

"Just tell me one thing," she said as she followed him back to the loft. "While you were dancing to that song, were you thinking of me? Or of Mooch?"

Justin grabbed a towel and snapped it at her. "Here, dry off," he said, passing her the towel. "I can't have you dripping all over my expensive carpets. And by the way, if you ever blab to a soul about what you saw, I'll tell all the housies about that tattoo on your butt."

"I don't have a tattoo on my butt."

Justin grinned deviously. "Maybe not, but how are you going to prove it to them?"

Kate laughed as she began to towel off her hair. Justin began a haphazard attempt to clean up, but as soon as he picked up a towel, Mooch saw the opportunity for a little tug-of-war action. With a sigh Justin obliged.

Watching them, Kate suddenly felt a delicious surge of pure happiness. She loved Justin so much. She loved that he made her laugh. She loved that he was silly enough to dance with his mangy old dog. She loved that he was tender enough to know when she needed his comfort and strong enough to give it. She loved that he was sensitive enough not to pressure her into having sex before she was ready and sexy enough to make her wish she *was* ready.

And maybe she was.

She had begun to dry her hair, bending at the waist to let it fall forward, when suddenly she noticed Justin's legs. He was standing in front of her. She stood up slowly, letting her eyes travel up his legs, over his flat stomach, his muscular chest, his shoulders. She met his eyes, and suddenly it felt like the air had been sucked out of the boathouse.

Justin took the towel from her hands and began drying her hair, gently, almost reverently. Then he worked his way across her shoulders, down her back, and knelt down to dry her legs, one by one, drawing rough terry cloth over smooth flesh.

Kate let her hands drift to his head, running her fingers through his hair and drawing him up to her. His lips met hers, soft and warm. His arms encircled her, pressing their bodies together.

Kate came up for air with a gasp. She started to pull away, but then she looked into his eyes, and something in her melted. She let herself relax in his arms, let him lay her back on his bed.

"You know you don't have to do this," he whispered.

"I want to," Kate heard someone's voice answer, slow and smoky. "Only . . ." Kate could feel his body tense, see the look of disappointment in his eyes. She had to laugh. "No, I'm not changing my mind," she said, kissing the corner of his mouth. "It's just that, you know, or I guess maybe you don't know—"

"What?"

Kate hid her face in the crook of his neck. "I'm not exactly experienced. I mean, I don't really . . . I mean, I've never actually done it."

"This is your first time?" He shook his head. "Boy, I guess the pressure's really on me to make it memorable, then."

Kate laughed and kissed the rough underside of his chin. "It's not that. It's just, you know, I don't have any experience. And you have. And there are all those beach bimbos crowding around your chair every day, and most of them probably know . . . you know."

Justin kissed her forehead. "You're the only beach bimbo for me," he whispered.

"Thanks. I think."

"Listen, though." Justin sighed. "I can't believe I'm saying this, but we really don't have to do this."

"I can't believe I'm saying this, either," Kate replied, "but yes, we really do. Really."

Kate felt Justin's hand slip her bathing-suit strap from her shoulder. "But first," she said, "I have to run to the house."

"Excuse me?"

"I have some things I need. You know, *things*."

"Oh," he said, nodding. "I was going to bring that up. Honestly. Any minute now."

Kate laughed and pushed him back. "I'll be right back."

"You'd better be," he warned with a grin.

Chelsea looked up at the sound of the front door opening. She was happy to see that it was Connor. He was wearing a sleeveless T-shirt, dusty jeans, and a dirty white hard hat that had a label in block letters spelling out his first name.

"You have your own hard hat?" Chelsea asked, laughing.

Connor nodded as he removed it. "It's no great honor. Simple survival. The fellows do occasionally drop something heavy."

"It looks very macho," Chelsea said with a wink.

"And how was your day, dear?"

"Pretty good," Chelsea said. "I took a lot of videos of people running around in the sand and splashing in the surf. My boss seemed happy. She says I have the perfect personality for the job."

"You just have the perfect personality, period," Connor said.

Grace offered up a groan, and Connor, looking embarrassed to have been caught in an actual moment of sincerity, added, "Great body, too." He headed for the kitchen. "And now I think I'll perform that ritual of construction workers everywhere and reward myself with a fine bottle of Guinness."

"Is that beer?" Chelsea asked.

"Actually it's stout. A proper Irish stout."

Grace used the remote control to raise the volume on the TV just a little. "You have an extra?" she asked Connor.

"It's my last one," Connor answered, shaking his head apologetically. Chelsea was certain he was lying. But the way Grace looked, she didn't need to spend another night drinking.

"You'd better look out," Chelsea advised. "Alec's in there trying to cook again."

Connor's shoulders slumped theatrically as he disappeared into the kitchen. Chelsea heard a loud, *"What the bloody—?"* before the kitchen door closed.

Just then the front door opened again and Kate came in, her face strangely ruddy. Her hair, for once, was tangled. Her bathing suit was still damp looking.

"Hey, Kate. Have a good swim?" Chelsea asked, yawning.

"Uh-huh." Kate headed quickly toward the stairs.

Chelsea cocked an eyebrow curiously and looked over at Grace. Grace, too, was eyeing Kate suspiciously.

"You know, I just heard on the news that the tropical storm has become a hurricane," Grace said.

"That's nice," Kate said.

Chelsea and Grace exchanged another look. "They also announced that there's a giant asteroid hurtling toward earth that will wipe out all life on the planet," Chelsea said.

"Oh, really?" Kate replied brightly as she took the stairs two at a time. "That's interesting. It's very interesting. I'll have to tell Justin." Then she paused, halfway up. "Not that I'll be seeing him. I mean, of course I'll see him—I mean, he lives here. Or at least he lives in the boathouse. So I'll see him, for sure. Only it's possible that someone else will see him first—that's why I was saying, you know, that I wouldn't necessarily be seeing him. Because . . ." She took a deep breath. "I have to go upstairs."

Grace shook her head as Kate disappeared. "I'll bet you a thousand dollars right now that she comes back down within sixty seconds, carrying her purse."

"No bet," Chelsea said.

There were loud footsteps on the front porch. Grace grinned slyly. "Must be Justin. He probably couldn't wait any longer."

But whoever was at the door knocked politely. "Justin wouldn't knock," Chelsea pointed out.

Grace sauntered over and opened the door. "Hello. What can I do for you?" Chelsea heard her ask.

"We're here to see our daughter."

fifteen

"Your daughter?" Grace repeated. "Well, you can't be Chelsea's parents—at least not without some amazing genetic accident. So I take it you're Mr. and Mrs. Quinn?"

"That's right," said Mr. Quinn, a trim, middle-aged man with gray temples and a solemn air. "I hope we're not interrupting anything, but we wanted to surprise her."

Grace felt a slow smile spreading across her face. "I can just about guarantee that you'll surprise her. Come on in. She'll be down any minute now."

Grace opened the door wider and stood back to let the two of them in. Chelsea, she noticed, was making a mad dash toward the stairs, presumably to warn Kate. But before she could get far, Mrs. Quinn cried out, "Chelsea! How nice to see you."

Chelsea froze in midstride and slowly turned. "Hi, Mr. and Mrs. Quinn," she said in a voice tinged with desperation. She glanced up the stairs, then toward the kitchen.

Mrs. Quinn, a stylish, brown-haired woman who had obviously been the source of Kate's looks, turned to Grace. "And are you Alexandra?"

"Alex . . . um, no, I'm Grace Caywood." Grace stuck out her hand. "I'm pleased to meet you."

"Kate's not here!" Chelsea blurted suddenly.

"But Grace said she was," Mrs. Quinn said.

"Grace!" Chelsea said. "Don't you remember that Kate went out to . . . to work with those orphans? Justine and, um, Alexandra and, um, what's her name, the other girl—"

"Connie?" Mrs. Quinn offered.

"Yes. Connie," Chelsea said quickly. "I don't know why I can never remember that girl's name. They're gone. All of them. Gone with the orphans."

Mr. Quinn looked suspiciously at Chelsea. "Orphans?"

"Uh-huh." Chelsea nodded. "So if you really want to surprise her, you should probably come back later, like around—"

Just then the kitchen door flew open.

It was Alec. Crying tears that ran down his cheeks.

Behind him came Connor, holding a brown bottle of Guinness in one hand and laughing openly at Alec. "Why do you think I had *you* cut the onions? Do you think there's no pain in cooking?"

Alec wiped at his eyes with the back of his hand. "Those aren't normal onions. They can't be." He ran into the couch, stubbing his toe. "Damn! I can barely see. I've been blinded by onions! You Irish bastard, you did this to me."

Mr. Quinn's eyes went first to the bottle of beer in Connor's hand, then to Alec's bare chest. Mrs. Quinn, Grace noticed, reversed the sequence.

"Oh, oh, oh," Chelsea sputtered. "These are friends of ours from another house. They don't live here."

"We don't?" Connor asked.

"No," Chelsea said through gritted teeth. "Meet Mr. and Mrs. Quinn. Kate's *parents*."

"Oh, right," Alec said. "Hi, my name's Alec. I mean, Alexandra. I mean—"

"Sex-change operation," Connor interrupted blandly. "The poor lad's very confused."

Mr. Quinn nodded darkly. "And I guess that makes you Connie? You a construction worker, *Connie?*" he asked with heavy sarcasm.

Connor nodded. "That I am. There's so many more opportunities nowadays for women like myself who want to go into traditionally male fields."

Grace snickered, but Chelsea's eyes just

grew wider and more desperate. Just then, they heard the sound of footsteps descending the stairs.

Kate was halfway down the stairs before she spotted her parents. She froze, a look of horror on her face.

"Surprise," Mr. Quinn said.

"Dad! Mom!"

"Yes, it's us," Mr. Quinn said dryly.

"We thought we'd surprise you, dear," Mrs. Quinn said.

"We've already met Alexandra and Connie," Mr. Quinn added.

"Oh," Kate said. "Oh."

"You know, it's funny, but there's really a very simple explanation for all this," Chelsea said quickly. "It's not at all what you think."

"Exactly!" Kate said. She headed down the steps, but on the third step her foot caught. She stumbled, clutched at the railing, and let go of her purse.

The purse flew through the air, landing at the feet of her parents.

Landing open.

Mr. and Mrs. Quinn stared silently down at the strip of square foil packages.

Then they looked up in unison at their daughter. Then they turned because the front door had opened.

"Kate?" Justin called out, looking somewhat disgruntled and impatient. "What's going on? I've been waiting forever."

"You!" Mr. Quinn said. "Aren't you the same beach bum Kate was seeing last summer?"

Justin's eyes flashed angrily. "The name is Justin Garrett."

Mr. Quinn pointed down at the pile of condoms on the floor. "Are *you* responsible for this?"

"No," Kate interrupted. "It's not what you think. Those aren't mine. I was just holding them for someone. Justin and I aren't . . . I mean, we're not . . ." She took a deep breath. "Justin just lives out in the boathouse, Dad. We're not involved or anything."

"Is that true?" Mr. Quinn asked Justin. "There's nothing between you two?"

"As of this moment, Mr. Quinn, that's true," Justin said evasively.

Mr. Quinn turned his gaze back to Kate. "Let's go, Kate," he said in an icy voice. He reached for the door. "We've got a lot of catching up to do."

Kate held tightly to the steel railing and leaned out. Turning her head right, she could see straight along the boardwalk. The buildings, all neon and bright colors from ground level, looked shabby and gray from the twelfth floor. The beach was empty now, and a warm, moist wind was blowing in beneath clouds that had brought the night earlier than usual.

"Honey, don't lean like that; you could fall."

Her mother's pleading voice carried out onto the balcony. Naturally, her parents had gotten a nice but reasonable room at the Ocean City Grand Hotel. Her father had explained that they'd snagged a good rate because the lousy weather had caused cancellations.

Kate turned her gaze left, where Ocean City petered out into empty sand dunes and beyond that into a national seashore park. One of these days she'd have to get up there, she thought wistfully. Maybe do a little hiking.

"Kate, I think you should come in now," her father said in a voice that suggested and commanded at the same time.

Reluctantly Kate turned away from the view. She stepped back inside. Her mother was transferring clothing from a garment bag into the closet. Her father was sitting in one of the uncomfortable-looking hotel easy chairs.

"Nice room," Kate said.

"We've been through all that, Kate," her father said wearily. "Sit down. We have to talk."

Kate did as he asked, taking a straight-backed chair by the round, glass-topped table. "What would you like to talk about, Daddy?"

"Oh gosh, I can't imagine. Can you, Marilyn?"

Her mother sighed. She hung the last of the garments up and sat down on the edge of the bed. "We just want to know what's going on, Kate."

Kate noticed the worry in her eyes. It was the counterpoint, the flip side, of the anger on her father's face. "I don't know what to say, Mom. You obviously know now that I'm sharing a house with some male roommates. I'm sorry I didn't tell you the truth. I should have."

Her father shook his head. "What you should have done is not come to Ocean City alone in the first place."

"I didn't. Chelsea came with me."

"You know what I mean," her father said.

"You know what we mean," her mother echoed.

But Kate wasn't sure she did. "Are you suggesting I should never leave home? That doesn't make any sense. In a few months I'll be going away to college. And I am eighteen," she pointed out. "You know—old enough to vote."

"Eighteen," her father said with a snort, "and look where you end up not a month after you move out—in some sleazy . . . some sleazy love shack."

Kate looked at them in puzzlement. "Are you saying you don't think I can handle living on my own?"

"You're living with that drop-out beach bum, and you've got a purse full of condoms," her father exploded, leaning forward in his chair. "That's handling things?"

Kate recoiled instinctively. She'd rarely seen her father angry. He was a gentle, rather quiet man. An intellectual. An academic type. "Daddy, I told you—"

"Told me what, that you're not sleeping with your lifeguard?" he nearly shouted. Then he took a deep breath and leaned back in his chair, visibly reining in his emotions.

Her mother took over, as if on cue. "Honey, we've always been there to listen. You know you can tell us anything."

Kate's first reaction was to agree. She'd deceived them for no good reason. If only she'd told them the truth, they'd have understood. Wouldn't they?

But doubt was gnawing at the edge of her awareness. Would they really have wanted to know the truth? They always said they did. She kept her eyes averted, staring down at a space on the burgundy carpet. "Remember how I told you about playing football that time, Mom? When I was thirteen and I played with some guys down in the park?"

Her mother stared at her blankly. "Sweetheart, what does that have to do with anything?"

"You told me not to do it anymore," Kate recalled.

"Just because we ask you to be honest with us does not mean we're going to condone everything you choose to do," her father said logically. "It was dangerous, not to mention the fact that contact sports with boys isn't a good idea for a young girl."

Kate hesitated, still staring down at the floor. "I did it again. Actually, I played a couple of times a week for the whole winter. I used to come home with muddy clothes and tell you I just fell down on my way home from school."

Her mother got up and went back to unpacking clothing from an open suitcase. "Why on earth bring that up now?"

"Because you wanted me to tell you the truth. So that's a lie I told you. Now I'm setting it straight."

A heavy silence stretched, broken only by the soft sounds of her mother piling socks neatly in a drawer.

"That's not the only lie I ever told," Kate said.

"Look, Kate," her father said, "we're not trying to attack you here. We're just worried, that's all. No one is saying you haven't been a wonderful daughter, someone we can both be proud of. You have."

"That's right, dear, we love you," her mother added, standing in the dusky light, holding several pairs of her husband's underwear.

"Top of your class," her father said, glancing back proudly at her mother, the two of them sharing a look of gratification. "Debate team, swim team, anything you ever tried to do, you did well."

Kate nodded, speaking now more to herself than to her parents. "I always wanted that. I wanted you to be proud of me." She laughed softly. "Chelsea's always kidding me because she says I'm trying to be the perfect daughter."

"That's not something to be ashamed of," Mr. Quinn said.

Kate looked at her mother. "Mom, you must have known I didn't fall in the mud on my way home from school. Not twice a week for half a year. You must have known I was going against your instructions."

"I don't think ancient history is the point here," Mr. Quinn interrupted impatiently.

"Ancient history?" Kate repeated softly.

"We just don't want any more lies, Kate, not from you, too," Mrs. Quinn said.

Kate closed her eyes and rubbed them wearily with the balls of her hands. There it was. There it was, as it always had been. "Mom, I'm not Juliana." She opened her eyes and turned slightly in her chair to be able to look out the window. Night had fallen, but no stars penetrated the blanket of clouds. "I'm not going to kill myself because I'm living with some male roommates. That's a little ridiculous, don't you think?"

"That's how it started with Juliana," her father said grimly. "With lies. Secrets. Friends she wouldn't tell us about. Boys she was seeing behind our backs."

Kate felt her shoulders slump. Darkness pressed so close against the window that it might have been painted black. "Why did Juliana kill herself?" she asked softly.

Behind her Kate heard a sharp intake of breath. Her mother. Kate turned to face her parents. "I've never understood," she said plaintively. "No one ever explained. It was all just platitudes—she was unhappy, she was depressed. Why?"

She looked to her father for an answer. To her shock, his eyes were wide with fear.

"I told you," he said. "It started with lies."

"Lies about what?" Kate asked.

Her father glanced at Mrs. Quinn, almost pleading.

"That's a very painful matter to go into right now," Mrs. Quinn said evasively.

"I thought we were all being honest," Kate argued. "I'd like to know. I need to know. I've spent all my time since that day trying to make up for what she did, trying to be the perfect daughter. I need to know why she killed herself, and what terrible thing you're afraid will happen to me."

"That's not what this is about," Mr. Quinn said. "No one is saying you'll go down the same path as Juliana."

"That's exactly what you implied," Kate pointed out forcefully. "It's what you've been implying ever since she died. It's why I have to be so damned perfect, so you won't have to worry that I'll end up like her."

Her father stood up. "Look, let's go downstairs and have dinner. I understand the food's pretty fair."

Kate just stared at him. "You don't know the answer, do you?"

"Are you ready, Marilyn?" Mr. Quinn asked his wife. "I'm starving."

Kate stood up, too. Suddenly, looking at her father, she thought he seemed smaller. He was avoiding her gaze, chiding her mother for being slow to get ready.

He doesn't know, she realized, turning the fact over slowly in her mind. Neither of them knew why Juliana killed herself. But surely there must have been some sign. Surely Juliana had given off some warning that she was in trouble. Had her parents been blind?

Or had they just not wanted to see?

"Did you even try to find out?" Kate asked. Neither of her parents looked at her. Her father straightened his sleeves. *They don't know. They didn't even try to find out because they didn't really want to know.*

"Ancient history," her father muttered under his breath.

A wave of bitterness swept over her, followed by a wave of sadness. Her parents didn't really want the truth about Juliana—or about Kate. They just wanted reassurance. That way they didn't have to cope or help or take responsibility. They weren't angry because Kate had lied to them about Justin. They were angry because, for once, they'd been forced to face reality.

"Before we go to dinner, there's one thing I have to straighten out," Kate said. "It's about Justin and me."

Her mother rolled her eyes. "Dear, your father is hungry, and you know how he gets."

Her father took her arm in his, drawing her toward the door. "As always, I'll have the two prettiest women in the restaurant with me."

sixteen

Grace felt weird not having to go to work. Not that she worked every night, of course. But this night she didn't have to go for a different reason. There was no work. No job.

No job, no David.

Tough luck for David. They could have been good together. Well, it was his loss. He'd have to look long and hard to find someone else like her.

Outside the window, the yard was bathed in darkness. No moon, no stars, nothing. Grace grabbed a beer from the refrigerator and flopped down on the couch in front of the TV. For a moment she debated changing clothes. She'd been wearing her blue silk kimono all day, and it was getting a little rank. But the idea of standing up again filled her with a daunting weariness.

She found the remote control and channel surfed until it became obvious that there was nothing better on than *Behind the Music* dredging up yet another story about David Cassidy. She watched it with the sound low. The words weren't important. She was feeling a nice, mellow buzz, her body melting into the couch, warm and tingly.

A green tennis ball rolled across the floor, and Mooch came zeroing in after it, his nails skittering across the hardwood. Alec followed. He was carrying a tall glass filled with a grayish-looking liquid.

"Hey, Grace. No work tonight?" Mooch brought him the ball and Alec reached for it with his free hand, but the dog refused to let go, shaking his head and letting out a low, very unconvincing growl.

"Nope." She looked Alec over speculatively. He was awfully good-looking, that was undeniable. Not really her type, but with those shoulders and that mile-wide expanse of chest, maybe she should overlook the fact that he probably lacked the experience and sophistication of, say, someone like David.

"What's in the glass?"

"Dinner. It's a protein shake—eggs, soy powder, bananas, wheat germ—"

"Please." Grace grabbed her stomach. "Spare me."

"Anyone else around?" Alec asked.

Grace tilted her head and let her eyelids droop in a gesture that she knew from experience made guys pay attention. "Just the two of us," she said. At least she could flirt a little, couldn't she? It was better than watching TV.

"Well." Alec pointed vaguely in the direction of the stairs. "I have to go and change."

"You have a date with Marta again?"

"No, not tonight. Some of the guards and I are going to check out a car one of my buddies is buying."

"Is Justin going with you, too?"

"He's down in the boathouse, working." Alec shrugged and smiled. "Something about mounting a winch."

Grace considered playing out her game with Alec. It wouldn't be hard. He'd certainly checked her out often enough.

She decided to let him off the hook. "Well, have fun," Grace said, turning her attention back to the TV.

Alec hesitated. "Come on, Mooch," he said. Mooch loped over happily, slimy ball in mouth. At the entrance to the hall, Alec paused and turned. "Grace?"

"Yeah?"

"Well, I was just wondering." Alec stared at the TV, avoiding her gaze. "I mean, I've just been noticing—"

"Speak, already."

"Is everything okay with you?"

Grace felt herself coil up like a tight spring. The last thing she needed was yet another temperance lecture, especially from Alec "My-Body-Is-a-Temple" Daniels, poster boy for family values.

"I just mean," Alec continued, fumbling and blushing like an idiot, "last night we thought maybe you were, you know—"

"I *was* you know," Grace snapped, "not that it's any of your damn business, and I plan to get even more you know tonight." She closed her eyes and waved him away. "Don't worry your pretty little head about it, Alec."

Alec cleared his throat. "Well, if you want to talk sometime—"

"I don't. Want to talk. Talk is not what I want." She opened her eyes to see what effect that had made, but she was talking to Alec's back.

Grace took another drink of her beer. Oh, well, maybe another time with Alec. Besides, according to him, Justin was down in the boat-house. If she wanted to flirt with someone . . .

She closed her eyes. It was easy to picture him, wearing cutoff shorts and a tool belt, intent on his work. No doubt fuming over that little scene with Kate. Kate, who didn't know what she had.

Yes, Justin would be brooding. Brooding and frustrated and feeling just the teeniest bit vengeful toward Kate.

She took another drink, finishing the bottle. Maybe she should pay him a visit. Bring him a nice cold beer, cheer up his evening a little. They could talk about old times.

First, though, she would have to change. She stood, wobbling a bit, and when she finally located her center of gravity headed for her bedroom. She rummaged in her dresser for the bathing suit she'd bought ages ago as a goof, knowing she'd never wear it out in public. It was a white T-back, nothing more than a few strings, really. She would just tell Justin she was on her way to take an evening swim in the bay. All very innocent.

Grace slipped into the suit and admired herself in the full-length mirror. David had no idea what he was missing. She pulled on a long sweatshirt—no point in shocking poor little Alec. Then she took a long swig from the faithful quart bottle of tequila by her nightstand, retrieved two fresh cold beers, and made her way down the lawn to the boathouse.

She knocked softly. Inside, she could hear the table saw whining. He probably couldn't hear her. Grace eased open the door and let herself in. Justin stood there, bent over the worktable, his back to her. Exactly as Grace had envisioned. He was wearing cutoffs, a tool belt, and a fine coating of sawdust.

She crept up behind him and ran one of the icy bottles along the muscles of his lower back.

"Dammit!" He turned, his eyes blazing beneath plastic safety goggles. "For God's sake, Grace, I'm using an electric saw. You want me to lose a hand?" He whipped off the goggles and threw them aside, staring at her carefully. "Grace, you're drunk as hell."

Grace just grinned and handed him a beer. He took it but didn't open it. "Are you going to lecture me now, too, Justin? Have you forgotten who I shared my first beer with one cold, winter day in a hollow under the boardwalk?"

"I remember," Justin admitted. He twisted off the cap of the beer and took a drink. "Still and all, Grace, you're getting a little out of control lately. I mean, I thought we both had gotten the drinking-till-we-puke thing out of our systems."

"I promise I won't puke," Grace said, crossing her heart. She took a step closer, standing only inches from him. "You remember what else I did for the first time under the boardwalk with you?"

Justin nodded. "My memory's pretty good."

"Mine too."

Justin shook his head ruefully. "Grace, why are you down here pulling your vamp routine on me? You know I see through you. You and I have been friends for way too long."

Grace laughed. "You're so sure of yourself, aren't you? Actually, I just came down to go for a little swim."

"Uh-huh. As wasted as you are? You'd hit the water and be out like a light."

"I know a lifeguard," she said coyly. "Maybe he'd give me mouth-to-mouth."

Justin sighed and rolled his eyes. "Racey Gracie. You haven't lost any of your moves, have you?"

Grace ignored the question. "I think a swim would do me good." She set her half-finished beer down on the worktable and slid the sweatshirt off over her head. There was no mistaking his sharp intake of breath. It made her smile.

"See? I told you I came down here to go swimming. I even wore my new bathing suit. Do you like it?"

"It's . . . it's definitely—"

She spun around slowly. "How about now?"

"Grace, I'm really trying to get some work done," Justin said.

She turned back to him and languidly wrapped her arms around his neck, pressing against him hard. She hadn't really intended to do more than flirt a little, but she was feeling so nicely buzzed. And Justin could probably help her forget all about David.

"Come on," she whispered. "It's not like I'm trying to get between you and Kate. It's just that, you know, maybe I could take some of the pressure off both of you."

"Grace," Justin said in a low voice, "you're just doing this because you're drunk."

"What do you care? You know you'll enjoy it. I know I'll enjoy it. What else do we need to know?"

A soft knock at the door made Justin jump back.

"Justin? Can I come in?"

"Kate?" Justin said loudly.

The door opened. Kate stepped in and froze. Her eyes swept the scene, lingering on Grace, then focusing on Justin.

"Sorry," she said softly. "I didn't mean to interrupt."

She began to close the door, but Justin moved to stop her, brushing Grace back against the table.

"Kate, wait," he said urgently.

To Grace's amazement, Kate paused. She

should have stormed out. She should have seen what was happening and run for cover. Instead she'd waited while Justin had dashed to her, pushing Grace aside as he went.

Grace felt like she'd been slapped.

"Kate, Grace is just a little—" Justin tilted his head toward the beer on the table.

"Polluted." Kate nodded.

"She—" Justin shrugged helplessly, as if he were embarrassed by the situation.

No, Grace realized, not embarrassed by the situation. He was embarrassed by *her*. Embarrassed by the way she was standing there, almost naked, her loneliness all too obvious. And Kate was actually looking away, the way she might if she'd walked in on some tacky domestic squabble. She was exchanging looks with Justin. Looks of pity.

Kate felt sorry for her. *Sorry* for her.

Grace wished she could shrink through the floorboards and disappear. She looked around blindly for the sweatshirt, located it at last, and tried to pull it on over her head. But the arms were twisted, so she just clutched it to her chest and ran, bursting between Kate and Justin.

By the time she fell face first onto her bed, she was sobbing, half hysterical from self-loathing and anger and fear. Her hands were shaking as she fished for the bottle, raised it to her lips, hating the taste of it and needing it more than she had ever needed anything in her life.

"Sorry about that," Justin said.

"Me too," Kate agreed. "Mostly I'm sorry for her. She was mortified. That can't be easy for a girl like Grace to accept."

"That's not all she needs to accept," Justin said gravely. "Grace was always just that little bit wilder than I was, just that little bit more interested in getting drunk and high. But I didn't know she would become an alcoholic."

"You think that's what she is?" Kate asked.

"I don't know. I'm no saint, so maybe it's not my position to say. I just figured she'd outgrow it. Instead she seems to be getting worse fast."

"Sometimes it's hard to see the trouble people are in. Even people you know well, maybe even love," Kate said sadly.

She could see that Justin was puzzled. But at the same time she didn't want to have to drag out the whole story for him. Not when she still didn't understand it herself. "Listen, I'm sorry about before. You know, when my parents showed up."

"They caught you by surprise," Justin said with a shrug.

"There was a lot of history tied up in that moment," Kate said. "A lot of baggage from my whole relationship with my parents, my sister . . ."

"Sounds to me like everything between you guys is pretty loaded," Justin said.

"And you only know part of the story," Kate muttered.

"Is there more to it?"

Kate bit her lip in sudden frustration. "I—I don't know. I have the feeling I may know even less than I thought I did. I just have the feeling a lot is wrong with me, with my folks, with the way we deal with each other. And I know that my relationship with you is tied up in it all, Justin." She sighed heavily. "Let's just say it's been a very strange night. Fortunately, they're leaving early in the morning."

Justin gripped her shoulders firmly. "Maybe you should take some time by yourself to think it all through."

"Yeah." Kate nodded. "Maybe you're right. Maybe I should figure some things out. I think I might call in and take the day off tomorrow. Take a drive somewhere."

"You know, Kate," Justin said softly, "you shouldn't be afraid to tell your parents you love me. That is"—he looked past her out the window—"if you do."

Kate looked into his eyes. "Justin, give me time, all right? Just a little, I promise. There's a lot I need to understand, but as soon as I do, I'll give you an answer that will be the truth."

Justin's eyes had grown moist, but he squeezed her shoulders in acknowledgment before releasing her. He turned back to his work.

"I'll wait," he said.

seventeen

Kate resettled the heavy backpack on her shoulders and ran her thumb under one of the padded straps, temporarily relieving the pressure. It was tough going, crossing the sandy soil. For every step forward she seemed to slide half a step back. But she reveled in the hard physical exercise. It was freeing in a way that nothing else could be.

She'd left her red Buick at the half-filled parking area at the park's entrance. It was unusually quiet. Probably the gray skies and stiff breeze. She'd been careful to make sure the top was up and firmly secured. She wouldn't mind a little rain, actually. It would keep the tourists at bay.

To make sure she would have privacy, Kate had hiked up along the shore through the scrub pines that in some places came right down to the ocean's edge. She estimated that she'd put a good two miles between her and the parking area, and it had been at least a mile since she'd seen another person.

The beach was narrowing, wedging her between the tree line and the increasingly agitated sea that was pounding the shore with the kind of serious waves you rarely saw on the East Coast. Overhead, gulls floated along, crying raucously at each other, at Kate, at the world in general.

A particularly large wave crashed and sent Kate scampering into the trees, fighting the stubborn branches that whipped at her face and clutched at her pack. She pushed on through the trees and came out on a short but surprisingly deep section of beach. The sand rose at a steep angle, foiling the efforts of the waves that crashed ferociously yet advanced only a few feet.

At the tree line she found a small clearing, a small pile of gray ash and blackened wood, showing that others before her had camped there. Not recently, though, and she doubted that on this gloomy, windswept day, anyone else would happen along.

Kate slung her pack to the ground and took a deep breath. The air promised rain. She took a quick swig from her canteen before unpacking her little blue nylon tent.

It took an hour to set up the domed tent, lay out her foam pad and light sleeping bag, and gather fallen branches and twigs for firewood. She was an experienced camper, and she fell into all the moves like they were an old, familiar dance.

Kate took a sheet from her pack and spread it out over the pine needles, weighting the corners with handfuls of sand. She pulled off her sweat-soaked T-shirt and sports bra and slipped into a bathing-suit top, leaving on her khaki hiking shorts. With a sigh she took off her well-worn boots and thick cotton socks and dug her bare feet into the cool sand.

Kate closed her eyes and listened. The waves gathered and rushed and crashed. The wind whistled through pine branches and skittered across the sand, slapping the taut nylon of her tent. A gull cried despairingly, and in the trees a squirrel chattered and scolded.

The air smelled clean, scrubbed, brand-new. There was salt spray, and pine sap, and driftwood. No hint of car exhaust, hot tar, cigarettes, or grease: the scents of civilization. No hint of suntan lotion, candy corn, and spilled beer: Ocean City's own special perfume.

Kate opened her eyes. The beach was still empty. The sun still tried vainly to burn through the thickening overcast. No footprints but her own marred the wind-smoothed surface of the sand. Perfect peace.

"Now I can think," she said aloud, shocked

at the jarring intrusion of her own voice. *Now,* she thought as she lay back and felt the breeze blow over her, *I can think it all through*.

She closed her eyes again, allowing memory to bubble up, the one intruder to this perfect place. Memories of a sister she'd idolized. Memories of hurt, confusion, anger. Memories that soon became indistinguishable from dreams, as the waves and the wind lulled her to sleep.

Grace woke up with dread. The instant she opened one eye and looked out at the gray-shadowed room, at the edge of watery sunlight that barely peeked around the corner of the shades, she knew the pain that was coming.

Her mouth was bitter and parched, her tongue thick. Her eyes throbbed as she slowly shifted her gaze around the room. When she stirred, the pounding in her head started. When she sat up, she felt the first wave of nausea.

Snatching at her robe, Grace ran for the bathroom. She got there just in time to fall to her knees and bend over the toilet, resting her forearms on the rim, shutting her eyes tightly while her insides heaved and twisted.

After a few minutes she stood up, trembling, and brushed her teeth to clean away the awful taste. When she spit, the toothpaste was bloodred. She dared a glance at the mirror. The eyes that returned her dull stare were puffy and unfocused, each vein visible. She felt even worse than she looked.

She desperately needed a handful of aspirin, but there was no way she'd be able to keep them down. Not yet, anyway.

Back in her room she found the bottle of tequila, now three-quarters empty. She twisted off the top and took a long drink. Her stomach heaved again, but she fought to control it. She needed the booze inside her to lessen the pain of the hangover. What was that saying? Something about hair of the dog that bit you.

The first drink stayed down, and so did the second. Now she could try some water, some aspirin, maybe eventually even some food if she was feeling brave.

Then the memory hit her.

"Oh no," she moaned. Had she really done that? Had she really thrown herself at Justin? And had Kate really seen it? Or was it all some vague imagining, something she'd seen someone else do in some other place?

She sank onto the bed and realized that tears were pouring from her eyes. She'd lost David. She'd lost her job. She'd made a fool of herself in front of Justin and been humiliated in front of Kate.

Was it any wonder she wanted to drink, with the beating she'd been taking lately? She had a right. Not like her mother. Her mother was just a drunk. Grace didn't drink because she needed to. She just drank because she liked it.

She swallowed another mouthful of the tequila and walked on uncertain feet to the kitchen. She poured herself a tall tumbler of orange juice and swallowed it down, then munched indifferently on a stale doughnut someone had left out.

Three aspirins and another glass of juice, this time spiked with tequila, and she was beginning to feel almost human.

"Anybody here?" she called out to the empty house. Good. She wasn't quite up to facing Kate or Justin.

The phone rang, a loud, insistent sound that sent shards of pain through her head. She stumbled toward the hallway and picked it up halfway through its second ring.

"Yeah."

"Gracie? It's me."

It surprised her to hear Bo's voice. "Hey, Bo, what's up?" She pressed the glass of juice and tequila against her temple and closed her eyes.

"You sound bad. What are you, sick?"

"I have a headache." *And every other kind of ache, too,* she added silently.

"I was worried about you, after last night."

Grace furrowed her brow. What was he talking about? "What?"

"Last night, when I called. You sounded . . . kind of out of it."

Grace shook her head. "You called last night?"

Bo was silent on the other end of the line. "I called and talked to you," he said in a flat voice. "You were wasted, weren't you?"

"No," Grace lied automatically.

"Mom forgets things, too, when she's drunk." This time he sounded more accusatory.

"I wasn't drunk," Grace said firmly.

"Mom lies about being drunk, too," Bo said.

Grace took a shaky breath. "Look, don't start comparing me to her, Bo. Okay, I got a little drunk last night. It's no big deal. It's not like I do it every night."

"Right, Gracie." His voice was soft.

"I'm telling you the truth, Bo. You know you've always been able to rely on me. You know that." Grace realized she was clutching the phone too tightly. Her knuckles were white.

"I know," Bo said. "I can rely on you."

"As long as we're clear on that," Grace said. She relaxed her grip and drew in a shuddery breath. "You want to come over tonight, hang out with me? Maybe catch a movie or something?"

"I guess not," Bo said. "I kind of told this girl I'd see her at the mall."

"Oh. Well, can't get in the way of romance, can I?"

"I gotta go," Bo said.

"Okay, kid. Look . . ."

"What?"

"Um, take care of yourself, all right?" Grace said, feeling the catch in her throat.

"Yeah. Bye."

Grace resettled the receiver in its cradle. Bo was mad at her. Mad at her for drinking because he was too young and too inexperienced to understand that there was a difference between the way Grace drank and the way their mother did.

He'd be okay. He'd get over it, forgive her in the end. Just the way Justin would forgive her for last night. And Kate. And David . . .

Tears welled in her eyes again, spilling down her cheeks and splotching the front of her robe.

She needed to get her act together. Take a shower, have a decent breakfast, see about talking Mike into letting her come back to work.

See about calling David, too. Maybe they could still get in a lesson today.

She brushed away the tears. "Get it together, Grace," she chided herself. "Sober up, deal with it one thing at a time."

On the way back to her bedroom she realized she was still carrying the tequila-spiked orange juice. She detoured to the bathroom to pour it down the sink.

Only Grace didn't want to pour it out.

She raised the glass and gulped it down hungrily. When she lowered it, she was smiling. Then she saw her reflection in the mirror, the expression of greedy pleasure, the raw need only temporarily sated.

And then Grace felt, more intense than the pain in her head, the new, fresh, stabbing pain of fear.

"Hey, you with the camera!"

Chelsea turned to look, but of course she'd already recognized the voice. Connor was sitting on the edge of the boardwalk between two other guys. They were dressed in a motley assortment of T-shirts, shorts, and raggedy running shoes.

Chelsea changed direction, heading toward him, shifting the weight of the camera and bag over to her other shoulder. With the thickening overcast completely obscuring the sun, the beach was half deserted. A real bummer of a Friday.

"What are you doing down here? Why aren't you working?" Chelsea asked, looking uncertainly at the other two guys. "There's not much sun to catch."

"We dug into a gas line that wasn't supposed to be there, so no more work until the gas company figures out what's going on," Connor explained. "Can't have all us dumb micks blowing anything up."

"Con's showing us around," said the tall, skinny redhead to the right of Connor. His Irish accent was even more pronounced than Connor's.

"This is Peter," Connor said. "He's newly arrived in America. And this is Tom. He works with me at the construction site. Lads, this is my very good friend Chelsea."

"Hi," Chelsea said, pleased at his choice of words. "Girlfriend" would have seemed sort of old school. But if he'd just said "friend," she'd have been hurt.

"Hi, yourself," said Tom, a burly guy with a touch of a beer belly and a mop of dark, unruly hair. He gave Chelsea a wry, somewhat unfriendly smile and looked her up and down. Suddenly she felt a little self-conscious. She had on her floral two-piece bathing suit, the one that always made her feel like she really ought to invest in some kick-boxing lessons. Around her waist she'd tied a sheer scarf, sarong style, but right now that didn't seem like quite enough camouflage.

"Three Irishmen on the loose," Connor

announced. "Tom and I are playing the welcome wagon. We promised Peter here that the sand would be covered wall-to-wall with beautiful girls in tiny bikinis. And look at it." He waved his hand at the near empty beach.

"I guess it's that hurricane. We're getting the outer edge of the clouds." Chelsea set her camera down on the boards. "Sure ruined my business. So," she turned her attention to Peter, wanting to be polite, "I guess you're from Ireland, too."

"Yes, miss," Peter said.

"He's coming to work with us," Connor said. "We had a sudden opening." He put on a devil-may-care grin. "Fellow name of Sean got pulled over driving without a license. The coppers turned him over to the Immigration, and by now poor Sean's on an Aer Lingus flight to Dublin. The idiot had a woman who wanted to marry him, too. He could have stayed in the country legally, but he said she was too much of a shrew."

"Sean was illegal, you see," Tom pointed out.

"She knows, Tom," Connor said. "And about me as well."

"Is that wise?" Tom asked, sharpening his gaze at Chelsea.

"I trust Chelsea," Connor said firmly.

"Trust? One of them?" Tom sneered.

"One of what, exactly, Tom?" Connor asked, lowering his voice.

Suddenly the beach seemed cold as well as dark.

"I didn't mean anything," Tom said, not sounding at all apologetic. "Only it's foolish enough to trust your own kind, let alone risking deportation just so you can try a little dark meat."

Connor bared his teeth in a tight, angry smile. He stood up, and when Tom didn't stand, Connor reached down and hauled him up by the neck of his T-shirt.

"Now, now, boys," Peter said, trying to get between the two of them. "Can't fight in front of a lady, now. It's uncivilized."

"Connor, don't," Chelsea cried.

But it was too late. Tom made a move, but Connor was faster. He smashed a fist directly into Tom's face. Tom sat down hard, his nose spurting blood onto the sand.

Peter made a grab for Connor, trying to hold him back, but suddenly there was another person involved. A blue-uniformed arm pushed Peter away and expertly tied Connor up in an armlock.

"All right, pal, take it easy," the policeman said. "Take it easy. Fight's over."

But Tom had recovered enough to jump to his feet and swing wildly at Connor. The punch slipped and struck the cop on the shoulder. A second policeman arrived at a run as a small crowd began to form. Peter faded away, backpedaling through the crowd.

Within seconds Connor and Tom were both spread-eagle on the boardwalk, facedown with their arms handcuffed behind their backs. More police were arriving, trying to get the crowd moving again.

Chelsea ran over to the first cop, who was rubbing his sore shoulder. He was young, not much more than twenty, an attractive black man. His name tag read Joe Stigers. Chelsea figured he was probably one of the rent-a-cops Ocean City hired each summer to handle the huge influx of tourists.

"It's all right, Officer, they were just playing around," she pleaded. She knew it was hopeless, but she had to try. Any minute they might demand to see Connor's ID, and then it would be all over. Just as it had been for Sean. Connor could be gone. Gone from her life in the blink of an eye.

"Hey, Chels. Hey, Connor."

It was Justin, slipping through the crowd. He looked down in some amusement at Connor, sprawled on the ground.

"You know this guy?" the first officer asked.

"Yeah, he lives in the same house as me," Justin said. "The other guy I've never seen."

"Tom's a friend of mine," Connor managed

to grunt. "A stupid, narrow-minded bastard, but a friend."

"Oh, well, then," Officer Stigers said sarcastically, "that clears it all up."

"We just got word, Joe," Justin said calmly. "Which means you'll be hearing about it soon. They're going to evacuate."

"What the—"

"Barbara's coming for dinner. The hurricane's turned. You know—the one everyone said would blow by us and we shouldn't sweat? It's heading straight for O.C. and building up speed."

"He's right," one of the other cops agreed, pointing to her walkie-talkie. "They just put out the word."

"Damn," Officer Stigers muttered, shaking his head grimly.

"You guys will have enough to keep you busy with Barbara," Justin pointed out. "And I'll vouch for these guys." He nodded at Connor and Tom.

Officer Stigers shrugged. "Too much paperwork to bother with, anyway."

Chelsea sighed with relief as he knelt down and unlocked their handcuffs. For the first time she realized she'd been shaking.

While Connor and Tom stood up, eyeing each other warily, Officer Stigers approached

Chelsea and pulled her aside. "Was this about you, sister?" he asked in a low voice.

There wasn't much point in denying it. The policeman wasn't stupid. "Yes," Chelsea admitted. "And I suppose now you have some problem with me dating a white guy?"

Officer Stigers looked at her seriously, then broke into a grin. "Well, I guess I'd rather have you go out with me, to be honest, but I don't mind if my competition is a white dude. I see plenty of hate between white and black. Why get upset over what little love there is?"

"Thanks," Chelsea said with feeling.

"You guys should get back to the house," Justin advised. "They're not ordering residents to evacuate, at least not yet. Just tourists. But you need to try to get the house ready for the hurricane. I'll get back as soon as I can."

"Hurricane?" Connor said curiously, rubbing his wrists. "Sort of a big storm, eh?"

Justin shrugged. "You might say that. When Hurricane Andrew hit Florida, it killed a couple dozen people and totally destroyed thousands of homes. Barbara isn't supposed to be that strong, but it's more than just a big storm. Make sure you and Kate and Grace all stay inside, keep the TV on, and do whatever they tell you to do."

"Kate!" Chelsea cried.

"What about her?" Justin demanded.

"She went camping this morning."

Justin's eyes blazed. "She's camping? Where?"

"I—I don't know," Chelsea said, swallowing hard. "She was hoping to find someplace secluded in the park. She wanted to camp by the ocean. Listen to the waves and think."

Justin's face went pale and grim. "Chelsea, by midnight tonight this beach, and every beach for a hundred miles, is going to be underwater."

eighteen

By the time Alec reached the clinic, the beach was nearly deserted. The sky had turned from overcast to ominous, layer piled on layer of steel-gray clouds, so huge, it seemed they could crush the frail city below.

All along the boardwalk, merchants had already closed up shop. Most were taping their windows, making big X patterns in duct tape across displays of bathing suits and T-shirts. Everyone spoke in hushed, nervous tones. It was eerily quiet, except for the steady crash of the waves and the urgent sound of hammering as some of the shop owners nailed up the plywood boards they usually reserved for the winter months. The boardwalk was rapidly taking on the look of a ghost town.

The clinic was brightly lit inside, the waiting room already full of patients from the surrounding area, many of whom had injured themselves in the hasty effort to shut down an entire city in only a few hours.

"I need to see Marta Salgado," Alec told the receptionist, leaning over the top of a shorter man with a crushed thumb.

"She's busy," the receptionist snapped. When Alec didn't move, she relented. "What's your name, and I'll tell her you're here when I get a chance."

"I can't wait," Alec said firmly.

"You have no choice."

Alec took a deep breath. "Actually, I do." He strode around the receptionist's cubicle and pushed open the door to the medical area. He spotted Marta immediately, bandaging the leg of a young woman seated on a gurney.

"Marta," he said.

"Alec?" she asked quizzically, glancing up only briefly from her work. "What are you doing here?"

"I came to get you. We need to get out of town until this storm passes."

Marta ripped a two-inch segment of white cloth tape and tacked the bandage in place. "What, are you afraid of big bad Barbara?"

"It's not that, Marta. It's just that it would be better if you . . . and me, too, moved to someplace safer."

Marta's eyes darkened. She looked up at

the patient. "There. Change that dressing every twenty-four hours and be sure to use plenty of Neosporin."

The patient hopped down and limped away gingerly. Marta turned an angry gaze on Alec. "No one has ordered an evacuation for residents," she said evenly. "So far, only the tourists are being encouraged to leave."

"That's because the Highway Patrol knows the roads can't even handle the tourists leaving, and they're worried about looting if all the locals split town. I heard that both highways are totally jammed. Barbara completely surprised the weather service. There was supposed to be no way she'd head toward shore."

"Well, then why should we try to leave?"

Alec knelt down so he could look her straight in the eyes. "Look, your dad sent me," he said gently. "He wants me to get you out of town. He's worried about you. Really, Marta, some groups of locals are being encouraged to leave town too. Old people, kids—"

"People with disabilities," Marta finished angrily. "I know. I heard the radio."

"Hey, it's not my idea," Alec said, his voice rising with a mixture of frustration and anger. "I work for your father, Marta. And this is what he told me to do."

"Fine. I'm refusing. Tell him that."

"He's got enough on his hands with this emergency. I'm not going to lay that on him now," Alec said. "Besides, I wish you'd leave, too. For me."

Marta shook her head vehemently. "That's not going to happen. I'm not going to be treated like one of the helpless. I'll take my chances. Besides, there's going to be work to do here at the clinic."

Alec stood up and glared down at her. "I could just pick you up and haul your butt out of here," he threatened.

"But you won't."

Alec tried glaring, but a wry smile forced its way onto his lips. "No. I guess I won't. But I'm sure as hell not going back to Luis and tell him."

"You know any first aid?"

"Sure. Red Cross certified."

"Well, you claim you want to be a doctor." She tossed him a roll of gauze. "Consider this a small step in that direction."

Justin tore through Alec's room, digging through his dresser and tossing underwear and T-shirts around frantically. Nothing. He ripped into the closet, pulling down a tennis racket, a half-deflated basketball, and a pile of paperback books, strewing it all across the floor.

"What are you doing?" Chelsea demanded from the doorway.

"I need Alec's Jeep. It's parked out front, but I don't know where *he* is."

"You're going after Kate?" Chelsea asked.

"If I can. The roads will be jammed. I need a four-wheel drive to have any chance at all."

Chelsea came into the room, eyes darting. Then she lunged for the beer mug filled with loose change on Alec's dresser. She upended it, spilling pennies, nickels, and dimes everywhere. "Here!"

Justin spun around and snatched the key from her fingers. "You're good," he said. "Remind me never to try to hide anything from you."

"Do you think she'll be okay?" Chelsea asked anxiously.

"I'm sure she's fine," Justin lied. "I'm just going to go and make sure. Will you be all right here?"

"Connor and I are storing up fresh water. There's plenty of food in the house, and we're moving all the furniture and stuff away from the windows. Only—"

"Only what?" Justin snapped, already halfway out the door.

"We can't find Grace."

Justin froze. "You tried The Claw?"

"They said she doesn't work there anymore."

Justin felt the blood pounding in his neck.

It didn't take much imagination to guess what Grace was up to. For days what she'd been up to was getting drunk. "Call her mom. Grace won't be there, but call, anyway."

"Justin, what if she's—"

"Look," he shouted desperately, "I can't go looking for her. She's in town, so she'll probably be safe."

It all sounded so logical when he put it that way, but the truth was he simply had to know Kate was all right.

"We'll look for her," Chelsea promised.

Justin ran for the stairs, descending them two at a time. At the bottom he hesitated just long enough to shout back up at Chelsea, "Call David Jacobs. The pilot. Maybe he'll know where she is."

With that he bolted and headed for Alec's Jeep. It started instantly, and Justin said a silent prayer of thanks that Alec had recently filled the tank.

There were a million places Kate could have gone to camp, but Chelsea had remembered her talking about the park. Of course, even then there were still hundreds of places to pitch a tent. He would have to get lucky to have any chance of finding her before Barbara bore down on Ocean City. And first he would have to get out of town past the hordes of beachgoers whose vacations had just turned ugly.

He pulled the Jeep into a U-turn and headed toward the boardwalk. When he reached Ocean Boulevard, he had to lean on the horn and all but force his way across the unbroken wall of cars heading one direction. All six lanes and both bridges were now one-way.

He finally found a way across, then gunned the Jeep down the side street, through an alley, and down another side street to the ramp that led up onto the boardwalk. Up, over, and the Jeep's tires bit into sand, spraying it behind him like a wake.

He turned north, racing at fifty miles an hour along the vacant beach, bouncing and bottoming out, sometimes even going airborne. The water was already narrowing the strand, the ocean turned almost black beneath low, swirling clouds that made early evening seem almost like midnight. Lightning was firing out at sea, again and again, jagged bolts arcing across the narrow distance between cloud and water.

Ten miles of beach ahead. Then he would have to get back onto the road to make his way to the park's first entrance. By then it would be pitch-black, and he would be searching for a needle in a very dark haystack, racing the storm that rushed eagerly to destroy.

* * *

The inside of the bar was a dimly lit oasis, far, far away from the giddy excitement and nervous anticipation of Ocean City. Grace sat at the far end of the bar, dressed in an expensively casual black cotton sweater and dark blue jeans with a thick cuff at the bottom. The jeans were for camouflage—her knees were scabbed from slipping and falling the other night.

She wrapped both hands around the short glass of scotch, gazing at the way the neon Budweiser sign over the bar reflected in the amber liquid. She took a swallow and felt it trace a slow burn down her throat.

Her mother's drink. Which just showed that good old Ellen had excellent taste, as usual. The scotch was far better than the tequila she'd started the day with. Richer, more complex, more satisfying. *Yep,* she thought, *old Mom has taste.*

The bartender slid her check in front of her. "Don't you think you'd better drink up and head on home, honey?" he said. He was middle-aged, dried-out looking, but not unkind. He'd looked doubtfully at Grace's ID, and after making a face that showed he wasn't fooled, poured her a drink just the same.

There were only three other people in the bar, a dive on the boardwalk called Petie's. A few stools down from Grace, an old man silently nursed a beer. A man and a woman sat at a table, drinking steadily and erupting into angry shouting every few minutes. There was a low stage at one end of the room where Petie staged bodybuilding contests, mud-wrestling contests, and anything else that would draw the boardwalk crowds through his door. Grace had never been in the bar before, but she knew it by reputation.

"I said, don't you think you ought to get on home?" the bartender repeated. "We're going to have to close up soon."

"Close? Why?" Grace heard the slur in her speech but no longer cared.

"There's a storm coming on, or hadn't you heard?"

Grace listened, concentrating for a moment on the sound of wind whistling under the doorway and rattling the black-painted windows. "So there is."

"A hurricane. Never had a hurricane this early in the season around here," the bartender said. "They say it happens, but I've never seen it. Maybe it's that ozone hole."

"Yeah, maybe," Grace said indifferently. She took another drink of scotch.

The couple got up to leave. The bartender called after them, "Hold on, I gotta unlock the door."

He turned the key in the lock and opened the door a crack. Instantly it was snatched out of his hand, slamming hard against the side of the building. A rush of wet, angry air swept into the room. Grace caught a glimpse of dark sky and a line of surf much closer than it should have been.

"That does it," the bartender announced after he'd wrestled the door closed again. "Everybody out. It's getting nasty as I've ever seen it out there." As if to confirm his concern, the building suddenly gave a long, mournful creak as the wind freshened.

The old man at the bar climbed to his feet and shuffled toward the door. He looked, Grace thought, like he'd be blown over by the first strong gust of wind. But that wasn't her concern. She wasn't concerned about much of anything, except the fact that she was going to have to leave her comfortable stool.

"You can stay, sweet thing."

Grace raised her head slowly and saw a huge man, heavily jowled, his shirt straining over the expanse of his belly.

"We gotta close up, boss," the bartender said.

"You go on," the fat man said. "I ain't leaving my bar."

"Whatever you say, Petie," the bartender said. He cast a glance at Grace. "Miss? You want me to see you get home?"

“She’s safe enough here,” Petie said, silencing the bartender with a look. The bartender shrugged and carefully let himself and the old man out the door, struggling to close it behind them.

Petie nodded at Grace. “What are you drinking, sweet thing?”

“Scotch.” Grace glanced toward the door. The wind outside screamed and made her jump.

“I think I’ll join you,” Petie said. He lifted an expensive scotch from the top shelf and poured them each a glass. Then he raised his, clinked it against hers, and said, “Here’s to Barbara, for giving me the opportunity to meet . . . what is your name, anyway?”

“Vicky.”

“Vicky. Well, good to know you, Vicky.” He tossed back his scotch, and Grace drank half of hers.

Petie eyed her closely, half closing his eyes. “You’re a beautiful young girl, if you don’t mind my saying so.”

Grace said nothing, just finished her drink and pushed the empty glass away. She pulled a twenty from her purse and laid it on the bar. “I’ve had enough,” she slurred. “Time to head home.”

She tried to stand, but the instant she

moved, her head swam. She clutched at the bar.

"I don't really see as you could do much walking," Petie pointed out. "Not in that wind out there." He refilled her glass.

Grace reached for it, but suddenly Petie pulled it away. "Hey, you know, now that I look at you, you might be a little under twenty-one."

"I'm twenty-one," Grace managed.

"Naw. I don't think so," Petie said. "And you're not named Vicky, either, so don't waste your time showing me some fake ID."

Grace reached for the scotch again, but Petie kept it out of her reach. A dull ache of fear rose through the haze in her mind. She should go, get away. Only . . . she couldn't walk.

"I've seen you around town during the off-season," Petie said, still sounding jovial, though his eyes were slitted like a lizard's. "I remember beautiful young women. I sure do." He shook his head. "And I remember seeing you. Always thought you should come in some night, try out in the mud-wrestling contest. You know we pay a hundred-dollar prize. You seem like you got the right equipment."

Grace felt like she couldn't breathe. The fear was growing, forcing the sluggish gears of her mind to work. But her head still whirled when she tried to slide off the stool and stand.

Petie leaned across the bar and stretched out

one chubby finger toward the front of her blouse. "You got the right equipment, sweet thing?"

"Leave me alone," Grace said, the words barely intelligible.

"Oh, come on, now. Let's not be unfriendly," Petie said, his voice menacing. "Here. You want your drink back?"

He slid the scotch closer. She reached, then froze, her fingers inches from the glass. Petie's finger had unfastened the top button on her blouse.

"Don't do that," she said, trying to sound firm.

Petie pulled the drink away. "You can't get something for nothing, sweet thing," he said softly. "That's bad business."

He slid the drink halfway toward her, just out of reach. She could lean forward and get it, but that would bring her closer to him.

He waited, nodding slowly, his mouth set in a smirk.

Grace reached for the drink, closed her eyes, and swallowed it all, wishing, praying, that it would bring her blessed unconsciousness.

nineteen

Kate awoke suddenly with the feeling that something was deeply wrong. The nylon tent flapped angrily over her head, snapping and tugging as if it were trying to break free of the stakes and ropes that held it down. The air was thick with humidity and tingly with static electricity. The crashing of the surf seemed unnaturally loud.

Then she felt the wetness at the bottom of her sleeping bag. As she sat up, she saw the water stain all around her feet. She stared stupidly at a small brown leaf of seaweed perched on her toes. How . . . ?

A wave crashed as if it were right outside—

Water exploded through the flap of the tent, green and foaming. It covered her, filled her mouth and nose, lifted her hair and swirled it around her head. She fought to reach air, but the tent was underwater. The shock of the cold made her gasp, giving up precious oxygen.

Then she felt the pull.

The tent was moving, twisting. She felt the scraping of sand beneath her, but it was liquid, offering far too little resistance. The tent was being dragged with the receding wave.

Kate fought to control her rising panic as she struggled blindly with the zipper of her sleeping bag. It stuck in the sodden material, refusing to release her.

She tugged the zipper back up to free it. Her lungs were beginning to burn. Her throat was convulsing, desperate to inhale.

The zipper slipped down, and she fought her way out of the soaking, leaden folds.

Suddenly there was air. She sucked in deep lungfuls. The tent settled around her like a shroud. Beneath her she could feel wet sand.

The second wave hit like a hammer, slamming her helplessly against the beach. She heard churning and the rattle of small stones and the scrape of nylon on sand.

Kate held her breath and searched with numb, shaking fingers for the tent flap. The nylon was like a second skin, glued to her, tugging her, tying her down below the water. She tried tearing it, but the fabric was too strong.

Her lungs were burning again. Time was running out. In a moment her body's reflexes would take over and she would breathe seawater.

Then, in a flash, she found it. The water swirled and opened the tent flap. She was through and clawing for the surface, shockingly far above her.

The Jeep bucked and shuddered, pummeled by the wind. Torrents of rain, flying nearly horizontally, cascaded down the windshield. The wipers were useless. It was like trying to hold back a waterfall. The headlights' weak beams barely pierced the darkness, swallowed up by the rain.

But Justin couldn't stop now. He had already checked out three parking lots for Kate's red convertible and come up empty-handed. Once a highway patrolman had tried to flag him down, but Justin had simply dodged around him, and the patrolman had apparently known better than to try to chase a fool in this weather.

Justin drove more by instinct than by sight, feeling the pavement through the steering wheel, praying he wouldn't smash into the trees that crowded both sides of the empty road. From time to time he felt the lurch and heard the bang and clatter as he drove over a downed branch. The only real illumination came from the incessant explosions of lightning that blinded him even as they revealed his surroundings.

Suddenly he stood on the brakes, and the Jeep fishtailed wildly before careening to a stop. Justin threw it into reverse, aiming the lights back to the spot where he'd seen the flash of chrome.

Yes! There it was. A red convertible, parked at the end of the lot.

As he pulled alongside the Buick, Justin fumbled under the seat for a flashlight. He aimed the beam into the interior of Kate's car. It was empty. He leaned on the horn but knew it was futile. In the screaming gale outside, the sound wouldn't carry more than a few feet.

"Which way did you go?" Justin looked left and right. The beach went both directions. Kate could have hiked either way. No matter which direction he chose, he would have to take the Jeep cross-country, through underbrush and trees in a night so black, he could barely see the end of the hood. The beach had long ago been swallowed by the sea.

Chances were he'd break an axle, or crash, or get trapped in some muddy ravine. Even if he chose right, the odds of finding Kate were slim and growing worse all the time. And if he chose wrong . . .

Justin closed his eyes, muttering a desperate plea that this one choice would be the right one.

He turned the wheel and aimed the Jeep into the woods.

Connor shoved Chelsea inside the house and with all his strength fought to shut the door behind them. A sudden shift of the wind slammed it shut so hard, it knocked Connor to the floor.

Chelsea rushed over, throwing her arms around him as he sat back up looking dazed and annoyed.

"Nobody warned me they had storms like this in America," Connor said. He patted Chelsea on the cheek. "I'm all right, I'm all right. Just bruised my bum."

"I still can't believe what it's like out there," Chelsea said, awestruck. "I mean, I used to *like* storms, but this . . . this is different. I thought that big tree in the front yard was going to snap in two."

"And the worst of it isn't here yet," Connor said grimly.

"Kate's out in that," Chelsea said, fighting back a sob in her throat. "And Grace, too, maybe." As if to comfort her, Mooch shuffled across the room and licked Chelsea's hand before retreating behind the couch.

"We did all we could to find Grace," Connor reassured her. "And David said he'd search as well. At least she'll probably be inside somewhere, unlike—" He fell silent and hugged Chelsea closer to him.

Unlike Kate, Chelsea finished his thought.

"Justin will find her," Connor said. "Besides, there's an old saying—God looks out for drunks and fools."

Chelsea managed a smile. "I guess Grace is the drunk, but is Kate enough of a fool to qualify?"

"I imagine that right about now she's starting to think so," Connor replied.

A gust of wind made the entire house groan as tree branches clawed at the roof. From far away came the poignant wail of a siren. Suddenly the lights in the living room flickered and went out, plunging them into darkness.

"So I guess we won't be watching the television," Connor observed dryly. "The electricity will probably stay out till the storm passes."

"I have a battery-powered radio up in my room," Chelsea said. The darkness was unnerving, magnifying each new sound. "I have candles, too. And my room faces the bay, so it'll be sheltered from the worst of the wind."

A bolt of lightning lit the room, a shivering blue that revealed Connor standing with his hand outstretched. In the blackness that followed, Chelsea reached for where his hand had been, touched him, and held on.

"Come on." He tugged lightly. "It's this way."

They walked in tiny, shuffling steps, reorienting with each new flash of lightning. Connor bumped into the hall table and cursed. Then he announced that he had reached the railing.

"Oh, good," Chelsea said, trying to sound cheerful. "It shouldn't take more than another hour or two to get upstairs."

"It's easy," Connor said. "Just go by instinct, and hold on to the railing."

He was right—the climb up was easy. Finding the door to her room was a little tougher.

"This is either my bedroom or yours," Chelsea announced as her fumbling hands found the knob. "Or the bathroom."

She twisted the knob and crept in, with Connor close behind her.

"Didn't I see this scene in some slasher movie?" Connor joked. "Two dumb kids creeping around a dark house, opening doors?"

"Ha! I found my bed," Chelsea announced.

"Good. I've been hoping to find your bed for some days now."

"That's good—keep up your sense of humor," Chelsea said. "Let's die laughing."

Connor bumped against her. "Oh," he said. "Sorry."

Chelsea felt her way along her bed, found the nightstand, slid her hands over the surface, and found the candle. Her fingers brushed a pack of matches, knocking them to the floor.

"Good move," she chided herself. "I dropped the matches."

"Wait for the next flash of lightning," Connor advised.

The storm obligingly provided a jagged bolt that filled the room with menacing shadows. Chelsea dived toward the matches and grabbed them, but as she did, she felt something cold and wet on the back of her knee.

"Connor!" she cried.

"That was Mooch," Connor informed her. "He followed us up. But thank you for that vote of confidence."

There was another flash of lightning, followed by a tremendous roll of thunder, and Chelsea heard a whimper and the sound of something crawling under her bed. "I do hope that was Mooch, too."

Connor sat on the bed, causing the springs to complain. "What's keeping the candle?"

"This matchbook is empty," Chelsea said. "There are more downstairs in the kitchen, but . . ."

"No, not likely," Connor agreed. "I guess

we'd better enjoy the dark, relaxing ambiance we have."

Chelsea sat beside him. She was very aware that her leg was touching his. But there was no way she could really concentrate on things like that when her friends were out in the middle of a hurricane.

The house was groaning and creaking more or less continuously now as the wind set up a constant scream, tearing at roof shingles and door frames and rattling the windows. Rain drummed on the roof and sheeted the windows. Chelsea could barely make out the bay, struck again and again by jagged bolts of lightning.

Still, she wasn't frightened. She knew she probably should be, but she felt safe here, with Connor beside her.

The springs creaked again as Connor lay back against her pillows. After a moment Chelsea lay back as well, letting her head rest on his chest.

They were all alone, together, cut off from the entire world. The house was empty and dark. All around them the storm was raging, but it only served to make Chelsea feel like she was wrapped in a warm, safe cocoon. She heard the beating of Connor's heart and felt the steady rise and fall of his breathing.

Chelsea tried to imagine where Kate was. She could be in terrible danger, or she could be safe with Justin. She might be afraid, but knowing Kate, Chelsea was sure she would find a way to deal with that. It was her duty, Chelsea reminded herself, to think of Kate and not to think of the way Connor's arm, wrapped around her, cradling her, made her feel secure and content.

"Do you think she's okay?" she asked softly.

She felt his sigh as a depression in his chest. "I hope so," he said.

Kate broke the surface and sucked in air that was still half water. Rain was lashing the heaving sea around her. The shoreline seemed miles away.

She began swimming, feeling utterly powerless in the grip of the enraged ocean. Her tiny arms were no match for the irresistible tug of each outgoing wave and no real contribution to the power of a breaker bearing down on the tattered beach.

It was less a matter of swimming than of surfing, she realized. She had to catch a wave. And then hope it didn't dash her brains out.

She felt the falling-elevator sensation as a huge swell rose up behind her. This was it. This was her only chance. She stretched out and swam with all her might, trying to match the speed of the wave.

It caught her, accelerating her like a bow firing an arrow. It was horrifying and exhilarating all at once.

The shore grew close at a terrifying rate. She could see that the waves were breaking clear up into the trees. The beach had disappeared. This ocean was eating the forest.

Trees loomed up before her as she hurtled helplessly toward them. Toward one tree. Toward one thick, black trunk.

She felt the scrape of rough bark along her arm, the sudden slam of earth leaping up to strike her. She tumbled and clawed at brown pine needles and handfuls of sandy dirt. She crawled, clinging at bushes that tore away in her hands, fighting the ocean's magnetism, resisting the irresistible.

Suddenly she was on land. Not dry, but not underwater. The edge of the wave seethed, but only a few inches deep now, harmless.

Kate stood up, then felt her knees buckle. She fell against a low branch and clung to it.

"Do you think we'll be okay?" Chelsea asked.

Connor nodded in the dark, the movement translated through his body. "Sure, we're safe enough. We're well above the water level and sheltered from the direct winds. Besides, I wouldn't let a storm hurt you."

Chelsea eased closer, letting her open palm rest lightly on Connor's chest. Through the barrier of his smooth cotton shirt she felt the heat of his skin and the rhythm of his heart.

She let her hand roam in slow, gentle circles. His heart was beating faster. Chelsea smiled to herself, savoring the moment. Amazing that her slightest touch could have such an effect on Connor. It made her feel sexy and powerful and maybe even a little bit scared.

Her fingers trembling, Chelsea slid her hand underneath Connor's shirt. She flattened her palm and let it slide over the hard heat of his stomach, the light dusting of hair, the smooth curve of his shoulders, resting at last over his heart. The wind still howled, the thunder shook the walls, but Chelsea could still hear Connor's shallow, labored breaths as he tensed beneath her touch.

She waited, barely daring to breathe herself. Even before he moved a muscle, she could tell he was about to reach for her from the sudden surge of his heartbeat.

He lowered his hand from behind his head, resting it on her shoulder, then leaned over and brushed her closed eyelids with his lips. Slowly he traced a path down the curve of her throat, trailing kisses like soft petals before finding her mouth. Chelsea felt a sweet shiver go through her as Connor let his hand slide down until the tips of his fingers grazed the side of her breast.

He stopped then, and she could feel him waiting for her signal, unable to read her face in the dark. Yes, she wanted to say. That much, but no further. Not yet.

She shifted her weight slightly, pressing herself against his outstretched fingers. His heart leaped. Chelsea smiled. It wasn't just a cliché. His heart had actually seemed to jump.

He found the buttons of her shirt and easily unfastened two, then reached for the snap at the front of her bra. The thought crossed her mind that this was not the first time Connor had done this. His touch was practiced as he twisted the plastic hook, opening her bra.

His fingers slid over her breast, and she felt a shudder go through her. His touch was perfect, dizzying, hypnotic.

It was magic, what she was feeling. She could lose herself in it so easily. Too easily.

"Connor," she managed to whisper.

His fingers stopped their delicious movement. She took his hand in hers and touched it to her lips, the same way he had kissed her hand not so long ago.

"It's not that I don't want to," Chelsea whispered. "I do. Believe me, I do, and never as much as I did two seconds ago."

"But you don't want to now?"

"The thing is," Chelsea said shyly, "the thing is, Connor, I'm not very experienced."

Connor laced his fingers through hers. "I don't suppose you'd be convinced by the argument that there's only one way to gain experience?"

Chelsea laughed uncertainly. "I guess I'm not ready for that much . . . experience." In a pulse of blue lightning, she saw Connor's half smile. When he didn't say anything, she kept talking. "It's not that I have anything against girls who do . . . gain experience. It's just that I was kind of raised to believe that sex was something you did with the man you married."

"Oh. I was sort of raised to believe that as well," Connor admitted. "But it's not my favorite belief."

A clap of thunder rocked the house, making both of them flinch. "All right, I'll believe it!" Connor cried in mock terror.

"Maybe I'll change my mind," Chelsea said, "but I don't want to decide just because we're here together on a frightening night."

"You'll let me know what you decide, then?" Connor whispered.

Chelsea gave him a kiss on the chin. "You'll be the first person I tell."

She nestled against him, and he pulled her close. For a while they lay silently in each other's arms, listening to the world outside.

"I wonder if she's okay," Chelsea said at last.

"Didn't you say you had a radio up here?" Connor asked.

Chelsea rolled to a sitting position, refastened her bra, and at the next illumination fumbled for and found the radio. She could find only one station, and it was fuzzy. Chelsea twisted the knob till the station came in clearly enough to make out. "I think they're doing hurricane news." She turned up the volume.

"There's a hurricane?" Connor asked.

". . . sustained winds of eighty miles an hour now in Ocean City, but it appears the city may have been spared the worst of it. . . ."

"See," Connor said cheerfully, "nothing to worry about."

". . . the worst of Hurricane Barbara, packing winds estimated at 110-plus miles per hour, has apparently come ashore just north of the city, striking the unpopulated area of the national park."

Kate huddled in the crook of the tree, shivering from cold and fear. She was drenched, her hair hanging down in her face, rain beating at her, bruising her with its fury. The ocean's edge still seethed and receded just below her. The entire world had become water and noise. The trees creaked and snapped with awful, tearing sounds. The waves crashed incessantly, pounding the shore without mercy. The wind screamed and howled and tore at her.

She clutched the rough wet trunk. She knew it was dangerous to be under a tree during a lightning storm, but there was no other choice. Not if she wanted to live.

Again the thought grabbed hold of her. If she'd moved slower, even by a single second, the ocean would have had her. One second to react and save her life. She had been that close to death.

The realization made her tremble anew. It would have destroyed her parents. Two daughters, both gone.

But then, this wasn't the first time she'd taken foolish chances. She'd never come this close, of course. But she'd always left her parents with the impression that the riskiest thing she'd ever done on her ventures into the wilderness was roast marshmallows around a campfire. After all, she'd gone rock climbing, white-water canoeing, even scuba diving in an underground lake.

She hadn't wanted to lie to them, but more than that, she hadn't wanted them to worry. They'd have tried to wrap her up in an envelope of safety and security. They'd have tried to protect her.

No, protect themselves.

The thought startled her. Yes, they had protected themselves, and she had gone along with the charade, convincing them that there would never be another Juliana in their lives. That the tragedy would never be repeated.

They hadn't known why Juliana died. They'd never wanted really to hear about Juliana's pain. They'd wanted Juliana to reassure them, lull them with the same comforting lies they'd demanded of Kate.

Kate almost felt like laughing. If she died here, her parents would never understand, any more than they'd understood Juliana.

A jagged bolt of lightning turned the world brilliant as the sun. In an explosion of thunder a nearby tree flew apart, the sparks quickly extinguished by the rain.

Kate screamed in terror, but the scream was just part of a vastly louder cry, the agonizing moan of the sky and the sea.

"I'm going to die," she said aloud, willing herself to accept it. There was no escape. She had no control any longer. All she could do was wait for the next bolt of lightning to find her.

It wouldn't be so hard, she told herself. It would be quick, too quick even for pain. Waiting in fear was the only real pain.

Maybe that's what Juliana had realized as she swallowed her little blue pills. That the only pain was in life, and that death was the end of all pain.

It was all too much for Kate to fight. The hurricane had decided to kill her. Its power was too great. The sea had missed, but the wind and the lightning would succeed.

The branch above her cracked suddenly, louder than a pistol shot. It fell, propelled by the wind, and slammed against her shoulders, knocking the wind from her. She fell the three feet to the ground. Lightning struck again, blinding, earth-shattering, splitting a nearby tree in half.

Kate sucked in air that smelled of electricity, refilling her lungs. She stared up at the bedlam sky, wildly agitated trees, and savage lightning.

"Nice try, Barbara," she said. "But you missed."

She rolled over and used the tree to pull herself into a sitting position and hung on like it was an old friend. Then she began to laugh, a mirthless, angry laugh. "You missed me, you bitch," she yelled. "You *missed* me!"

* * *

Justin heard the scrape of the tree trunk grinding along the side of the Jeep, peeling away whatever was left of the paint. Branches scrabbled at the underside. The wheels lurched, and the seat delivered a relentless beating to his body.

He had no idea how far he had gone. It was impossible to judge distance, and time was measured not in minutes but in deadly flashes of lightning.

He gunned the engine, climbing out of one more wet depression, twisting the wheel to slide past one more tree trunk looming suddenly out of the pitch-black hell around him.

And then he saw her, a wispy, indeterminate figure, suddenly illuminated by a flash of blue, and his heart stopped. He turned the wheel until the headlights found her again.

She was standing. Clutching at a tree trunk, leaning against the wind. And as he watched, she tilted back her head and shouted up at the sky.

She was screaming at the storm, defiant and unafraid. And Justin knew that if he lived a hundred years, he would never forget that moment.

He opened the door, using every muscle to fight the wind. He staggered out, nearly flattened by the onslaught. In a split second he was drenched. It took many seconds to reach her, to touch her cold hand.

He wrapped her in his arms, neither of them able to speak in the chaos. Slowly they made their way, holding each other, battling the wind, clawing their way back to the Jeep.

Then suddenly they were inside, the rain pelting the thin roof.

Justin turned on the heater.

"You found me," Kate said at last, breathing slowly, tentatively, as if she had forgotten how.

"You're alive," Justin said.

Kate nodded. "I almost gave up."

"But you didn't."

She looked at him, still shivering but her eyes ablaze. "No, I didn't. I'm sorry she gave up, but I can't change that."

Justin nodded. He knew who she meant. "No, you can't."

Kate was silent for a long time. Justin pulled a blanket from the back and wrapped it around her. At last Kate looked at him again. "It almost got me, but I decided I wasn't going to let it. I fought for my life." Her voice broke. "I was so scared, but I fought back."

Justin waited silently, his heart too full for words.

"From now on, this is my life," Kate said, her voice growing stronger. "I fought for it, and it's mine."

Justin smiled and brushed away a tear. "You

know we can't get out of here tonight. We'll have to ride it out here in the Jeep."

Kate brightened, momentarily her old self again. "Hey, it's the lap of luxury. Only right now I have to go to sleep. All right?"

"All right," Justin said, stroking her wet hair.

She had barely reached the back of the Jeep when she collapsed into sleep.

twenty

Alec stepped out onto the boardwalk, stretching up high, his arms over his head. He gazed at the sky and was surprised to find it nearly clear, as though what it had done last night was all some terrible mistake and now it was ready to apologize.

Marta stopped her chair by his side. "What a night," she said.

"Dr. McGraw says we handled thirty-two patients before the storm hit, ten during, and nineteen so far this morning," Alec said. "You, me, and the doctor."

"We're the best," Marta said, smiling wearily.

"And we survived Hurricane Barbara."

Alec surveyed the beach. It was littered with driftwood, seaweed, and other washed-up debris. Two lifeguard stands had simply disappeared, toppled and hauled away like prizes by the storm surge. But the boardwalk had escaped most of the fury, and already, relieved shop owners were sweeping up the shards of glass from their windows and thanking providence that the waves had stopped where they did.

"Well, I'm ready to get out of here and get some sleep," Marta said. "Can we take your Jeep?"

Alec shook his head. "No, it's back at my house. Why don't we take the scenic route, see what the rest of the boardwalk looks like?"

"Because I'm way too tired to push myself that far," Marta admitted.

"I'm feeling kind of wide awake myself," Alec said. "I'll drive." He took the handles of her chair and began to push her along at a relaxed pace. "You know, your dad is going to kill me when he finds out I didn't get you out of town."

Marta laughed. "If you promise not to tell anyone, I'll let you in on a big secret."

"Really? That sounds enticing."

"My dad's been scaring lifeguards with his tough-guy act for years," Marta said, stifling a yawn. "He's really the sweetest guy in the world."

"If you say so," Alec said.

"You don't believe me?"

"Nope."

Marta laughed. "You're not so dumb, you know that?"

* * *

Grace woke when her teeth crunched on sand. She spit with a dry mouth that felt swollen and thick. When she pried open one eye, she saw her arm stretched out before her, half buried under the sand. Thin stripes of sunlight gave her skin a zebra pattern. She rolled her eye upward and saw wide, rough-hewn boards less than a foot above her head.

It was as if she were in a wooden crate containing only sand and her own aching, bruised body. Then she heard sounds—hammers pounding, footsteps, and loud, cheerful voices. Through the cracks between the boards she realized she could see narrow slivers of brilliant blue and shadows cast by people walking over her.

She was under the boardwalk. Only she had no idea how or when she had gotten there. Her left arm had gone to sleep. Her head was a mass of throbbing pain. Her ears rang. Her vision swam. Her body refused to move when she gave it weak, uncertain orders.

Above her, people were talking. "Yeah, we were lucky," one man said. "Tourists will be back by Tuesday," another voice predicted confidently. "No one killed, thank God," a woman's voice chimed in, "just a lot of broken windows and a couple of roofs torn off."

Grace felt her attention waver. It was

impossible to put any of it in context. She was dizzy and nauseous. If she tried, she might remember how she'd come to be here, invisible beneath the boardwalk, but some instinct warned her that she didn't want to press her memory too far.

Another voice reached her ears, a man's voice, familiar but from far away, another time and place. "Have you seen this girl?" he asked. "She's been missing since before the storm." "A pretty girl," said a woman's voice. "Yes," he answered, "yes, she's beautiful. Her name is Grace. Call her friends at this number if you happen to see her."

Grace heard David walk away, his slow footsteps passing right over her. And the woman's voice said, "I sure hope that girl of his is all right. I'd hate to think the storm really did get someone after all."

"Pretty girl like that always comes through okay," a man said, and laughed reassuringly.

Grace wanted to cry, but it was too much effort. Instead she simply relinquished consciousness, letting her cheek settle again on the moist sand.

Kate reached for Justin but pawed empty air. She sat up, wincing at the stiffness in her neck and back, and looked around. The rear windows of the Jeep were milky plastic, but she could make out a moving shape outside.

She climbed out of the back of the Jeep gingerly, being careful of her tender, bruised body. She looked around in wonder. Dozens of trees were split and charred by lightning strikes or cracked in half by the sheer brute force of the wind. Most were bare; only a few stubborn pine needles had managed to ride out the storm. Pools of water sat in every low point in the ground.

But the ocean had decided to return the beach, withdrawing to reveal the golden sand again. And except for a few scattered puffs of white, the sky was clear. The air was sweet and clean.

Justin was down at the far end of the beach, wading through the surf in his shorts. He was carrying something muddy in his hand. Kate waved, and he waved back, hurrying his pace.

Kate tilted back her head, drinking in the feel of the sun. She was sore and hungry and ached in every joint, but she felt absolutely alive, as if she were plugged into some inexhaustible power source. She was solar powered, absorbing energy straight from the sun. She could run a thousand miles, she could swim the ocean, she could, if she wanted, fly straight up into the air.

"Hey," Justin called as he got closer, a huge

grin on his face. "How do you feel?" He tossed aside the object he was carrying.

"I feel . . ." She spread her arms. "I feel great. I feel like . . ." She shook her head and laughed joyously.

Justin ran and caught her up in his arms. "Surviving a close brush with death seems to be quite a little pick-me-up."

She laughed again and hugged him and danced away. "If I don't move, I'm going to blow up," Kate said, running backward until he started after her. She turned and raced away at full speed, stretching out her long legs, pumping her arms, exulting in the feel of clean wind in her hair and the wet sand beneath her feet.

She splashed through the water and plunged headfirst into a gentle wave, twisting around underwater like a dolphin doing tricks. When she came up for air, she tossed back her head and let out a shout of pure, undiluted happiness.

Justin was still on the shore, watching her contentedly, letting her have this moment all to herself.

"I'm alive," Kate whispered. "I made it. I won."

She tried a backward somersault and was rewarded with a mouthful of salt water. She came up sputtering and giggling, then deliberately sucked in a big mouthful of seawater and squirted it out like a fountain.

"So basically, you're feeling pretty good?" Justin called, grinning and shaking his head.

Kate climbed up the beach. She couldn't seem to stop smiling, and she didn't even want to try.

"Look." Justin held up the muddy object he'd been carrying before.

"My backpack," Kate cried. "Where did you find it?"

"Far end of the beach, wedged about ten feet up in a tree. A little apology from Barbara, I guess."

Kate snatched the pack and untied the drawstring. "Hey, my purse. And food! A Snickers bar. A very wet Snickers bar."

"Food would be nice," Justin acknowledged. "It'll take us an hour at least to get Alec's poor Jeep out of here."

Kate started to set the backpack aside, but then she stopped. She reached in and unsnapped her purse instead.

Slowly she felt a very different kind of smile spread across her face.

She set the backpack down and raised her eyes to Justin. He stood, waiting patiently, eyeing her curiously. "You came to save me," Kate said.

Justin shrugged. "I'm a lifeguard."

Kate stepped closer. She saw the way

Justin's gray eyes opened wide. "How can I ever thank you?"

"Well, I . . ."

"Don't argue, all right?" Kate said, stepping closer still.

"You've had a bad night," Justin said gently. "Maybe you should think this over."

"You think I'm just stressed out?" Kate asked, softly mocking. She touched his side. The hard muscles there quivered in response. "That's not it, Justin."

He gave up resisting and raised his hand to her cheek, his touch as gentle and warm as the breeze. "I just thought I'd give you a chance to change your mind," he said.

"I don't want a chance." Kate lifted her T-shirt off with both hands in one swift move. The sun was warm on her breasts.

Justin moved closer, slowly pressing his chest against her. Thighs skimmed, hips brushed, fingers laced. His skin was smooth and hot. "Are you saying—"

"I'm saying that I love you, Justin." Kate released his hand and traced the rough edge of his jaw with her fingertips. "And that I want you." She drew back just an inch, giving him a sideways look. "That is," she added, smiling, "if you're still interested."

His answer was a kiss, urgent and deep,

sending a new, dangerous, intoxicating feeling to join the heady joy already bursting within her.

Slowly he lowered her to the sand. He kissed her again, and she heard herself moan softly. Kate let her hands roam over the hard ridges and curves of his body, smooth and sculpted as a dune. She knew it all so well, but this time he felt new to her. Each kiss tasted of adventure and joy and something sweet and pure that she knew was love.

She did love Justin, she always had, and she probably always would. And he loved her. She could see it in his tender smile, feel it in his touch. This was right for her. And from now on, she was doing what was right, for her, and only for her.

They exchanged a secret smile, and Kate felt glad that they were going to make love here, in this very special, private place, not in the dark, but with the hot caress of the sun on their bodies. When all their clothes were tossed aside, Justin gazed at her, mesmerized, like the witness to a miracle, and then he reached for her.

"I need my purse," she said, feeling awkward for the first time.

Justin rolled his eyes. "Great time for a candy-bar fix," he teased. He grabbed her backpack and handed it to her. She searched through her purse and found the gold foil packets.

Justin reached for one. "Was there some reason you brought these camping with you?"

Kate laughed. "Same reason I brought the candy bar. You never know when you might get a sudden craving."

Justin grabbed her playfully, but when his eyes locked on hers, he fell serious again. Gently he laid her back against the sand. His lips traveled down her neck, grazing her collarbones, featherlight at first, then more intense. She closed her eyes, savoring the lush, lazy heat in her veins as he explored her body, searching and learning.

For a long while she listened to the waves, lapping gently, sometimes louder, sometimes barely audible, and then it was only Justin's voice she heard. "I love you, Kate," he whispered. She felt his lips on hers, and then she was caught up in something stronger than the thunder and the wind of the hurricane.

twenty-one

When Kate and Justin drove up to the house, they found Alec trudging across the lawn, looking tired and grumpy.

"Uh-oh," Justin said. "I've been afraid of this."

Kate raised her head from his shoulder and made an effort to erase the dreamy smile she knew was on her lips. "The love shack looks okay," she said.

"The what?"

Kate smiled. "That's what my father called it. A 'love shack.' Actually, a 'sleazy love shack.' "

"It is not sleazy," Justin said. Then he winced as he saw Alec stop dead and stare openmouthed at the Jeep. "I guess it's too late to try to run away." With a sigh he opened the door and climbed out.

"My Jeep," Alec muttered, shaking his head slowly as Kate joined Justin on the sidewalk.

Justin scratched his head and looked down

at the ground. "Yeah, well, I had to kind of borrow it."

"My Jeep," Alec repeated.

"Had to do a little cross-country driving, and I was kind of in a hurry," Justin explained. "The paint got a little scratched."

Kate turned to look back at the Jeep. It had once been red. Now most of it was a two-tone affair, part bare steel, part rust-colored primer coat. A two-inch-deep dent had crumpled the hood. The front bumper was clinging on, but just barely. The vertical grille was missing two teeth. Through the gap, steam hissed from the punctured radiator. The canvas top was slashed in several places, and the left headlight had suffered a direct hit.

"My Jeep," Alec repeated blankly. "What . . . my . . . what . . . it's my—"

"Yeah, well, I hope you have insurance," Justin said, "or I'll have to spend the next three months working to pay for it to be fixed." He handed Alec the key. "Here. I guess it won't help if I promise never to borrow it again, huh?"

When Alec didn't answer, Kate walked over to his side. "Thanks, Alec," she said, patting him gently on the shoulder. "You can borrow my convertible anytime. That is, if you're careful with it."

Alec's hand dropped to his side, the key clinking on the sidewalk.

Justin turned to Kate. "We'd better get inside before he snaps out of his trance and comes after me with a crowbar."

Chelsea and Connor were sitting side by side on the living-room couch, sipping tea and watching news coverage of the hurricane. The instant she saw Kate, Chelsea leaped to her feet and hugged her so hard, Kate thought she might pass out.

"You're back, you're back!" Chelsea screamed. "You made it!"

"Yeah, amazing, huh?" Kate said happily.

Chelsea held her out at arm's length. "Are you really okay?"

"I'm really okay," Kate promised.

Chelsea looked into her eyes, cocked her head, then looked again. "You look okay," she said.

"Really, I'm fine," Kate assured her again.

Justin spread his hands. "No one even cares how I am," he grumbled.

Connor saw his cue, jumped up, threw his arms around Justin, and did a note-perfect imitation of Chelsea's happy squeal. "You made it," Connor cried. "Oh, happy day!"

"Oh, shut up." Justin pushed him away.

Chelsea was still staring at Kate, her lips

pursed in concentration. "There's something else going on with you," she said. "You look *more* than okay."

Kate felt the grin spread across her face.

"That's not an I-survived-a-hurricane grin," Chelsea said. "No, that's some completely different kind of grin."

"Did you guys find Grace?" Justin asked.

Instantly the mood grew darker. Connor shook his head. "We searched till the storm got too bad and went back out again this morning. David's been out, too. We found some pictures of her in her room when he came around this morning. He's showing them up and down the boardwalk."

Kate slipped her arm through Justin's. "She'll be all right, I'm sure. We'll go right out and look as soon as we get a chance to eat something."

"We were about to go out, too," Chelsea said. She bit her lower lip. "Maybe we should have talked to her, tried to get her some help, Kate."

Justin shook his head firmly. "She wasn't ready to listen, Chels. Trust me."

Chelsea sighed. "At least the two of you are back safe and sound. When we heard on the radio that the worst of the hurricane hit right where you were . . ." Her voice broke, but she recovered quickly. "Not that you seem to have come out of it too badly," she added.

Chelsea let out a long sigh. They'd been searching the boardwalk for hours without success, scanning the faces in the thin crowd out celebrating the town's survival. Everyone except Chelsea and Connor seemed to be in a good mood, breathing a collective sigh of relief that they'd survived the storm. Shop owners leaned in their doorways, smiling and nodding at passersby. Even the usually impertinent gulls were on their best behavior, huddling quietly on the storm-battered beach.

Chelsea found her mind wandering back again to the subject of Kate and Justin. "You know they did the deed," she said to Connor.

"What are you talking about?" Connor asked distractedly. "Who did what?"

"You are such a guy," Chelsea said, shaking her head despairingly. "Kate and Justin. It was obvious."

"Come again?"

"They did it. *It*. A blind person could see it."

"What, you mean they had sex?" Connor asked slowly.

"Duh."

"I assumed they were doing it all along,"

Connor said reasonably. "Is that her?" He pointed at a tall girl a few yards ahead of them on the boardwalk.

"No. Too tall, and the hair's the wrong color." Chelsea shook her head. "It was the first time."

"Not for him," Connor said with a laugh.

"For her."

"Well. Should we send her congratulatory flowers or sacrifice a lamb or something?"

Chelsea punched his arm. Then she relented and wrapped her arm around his waist. Who cared if some of the eyes passing them held expressions of disapproval? Others made a point of smiling, she'd noticed.

"Are you mad at me for saying no?" Chelsea asked after a while.

Connor thought it over for a moment. "Never gave it a second thought."

"You liar."

"Of course I'm not angry," he said, pulling her closer. He laughed. "I did take a very cold shower this morning."

"Like you had a choice. We didn't *have* any hot water."

Chelsea fell silent. There was something she wanted to say, and she didn't want to think about it too hard, or she was afraid she'd lose her nerve.

Besides, she'd thought about it all night as they had lain in each other's arms and listened to the wind trying to smash its way into the house. She couldn't lose Connor. She was in love with him. At least, she thought she might be. And if he were snatched away, well, she'd never have the opportunity to be certain.

"I do care about you," she said, feeling her way tentatively. "A lot. And I worry about you getting deported. I don't think I could stand that."

"I'm not keen on it myself," Connor agreed.

"Anyway, when you and your friends were talking yesterday," Chelsea continued, forcing out the words before they got caught in her throat, "you said something about a friend of yours who could have gotten married and stayed here in America."

"Sure, it's fairly common," Connor replied as he stepped over a pile of debris. "Marry an American citizen, and as long as it doesn't look too phonied up, you can get a green card."

Chelsea took a deep breath and let it out slowly. "I would really hate to lose you," she said, locking her eyes on the calm waves in the hope of calming herself. "Connor, maybe you won't like this idea, but we're both Catholic, so at least we're the same religion, even if we're slightly different colors—"

Connor stopped and put a hand to her lips. When she tried to speak again, he kissed her mouth.

"Are you trying to shut me up?" she asked, pulling away.

"You won't sleep with me, but you *will* marry me? Is that where you're leading?"

Chelsea shrugged. "After we got married, I'd definitely sleep with you."

Connor laughed, but Chelsea could see that his eyes were serious. "I won't let you make this sacrifice to save me," he said flatly.

"It wouldn't be such a sacrifice," she said.

"No, it wouldn't," he agreed quietly. "I do adore you."

"Well, I feel the same about you."

Connor stroked her cheek. "Chelsea," he said with a sigh, "there are so many things you don't know about me."

"So? I like a man of mystery." But she knew he was right. Connor rarely talked about his family, and he hardly ever mentioned his life back in Ireland. Still, there'd be plenty of time for all that down the road.

"No." He shook his head firmly. "No. It's out of the question."

"Don't I have a say in this? Besides, it's not like we have to tie the knot tomorrow."

He looked at her with a faraway smile.

"Maybe someday, then. Let's leave it at that, eh?"

"I was thinking more like we give it a week."

"A week?" Connor exclaimed.

"You know. Seven days."

Connor shook his head. "A week, then. So be it. And if you want to forget you ever brought it up, I'll understand." He kissed her again, a slow, sweet kiss that left her wishing for more. "Of course, we could just skip ahead to the honeymoon," he teased.

"And how exactly would that help your immigration status?"

"It would help me sleep at night," he grumbled as they started to walk again, swinging their hands back and forth.

Chelsea raised her eyebrows. "I don't know," she said, grinning. "I kind of like the idea of you in the next room, unable to sleep."

"All right, wake up and come on out of there."

Grace woke up sliding. Someone was dragging her, holding on to her ankle. She struggled, trying to resist, but her hands just grabbed at sand.

The boards slid by above her and then she

was on her back, staring up at the remnants of a stunning sunset.

The flashlight shone on her face again. "All right, stand up, miss." The voice was no-nonsense but not unkind. She made an effort to comply, rolling over and managing to rise to her knees.

"You'll have to do better than that, or we'll need to take you in to dry out," the policeman said.

He reached down and lifted her by the arm. Grace forced her numb legs to work and stood, fighting to stay erect.

"What's your name, miss?" the policeman asked.

Grace raised a hand to ward off the sharp glare of his flashlight. He switched it off. "What's your name, miss?" he repeated.

She tried to answer, but her mouth was as dry as cotton, and nothing came out but a hoarse whisper. She tried again, consciously forcing her parched tongue to work. "Grace," she whispered.

"Grace. Well, Grace, you look like you had a better time last night than most people in this town. You been drinking?"

Lying was just too difficult. It was hard enough to answer at all. She nodded.

"Figured."

She started to slump to the ground again, and the policeman caught her. "Miss," he said firmly, "if you can't stay on your feet, I'll have to take you down to the drunk tank, and I don't want to have to do that to you. It's not a nice place."

Grace nodded. "I'm okay," she whispered.

He released her and took a step back. "No, miss, you are definitely not okay."

"Just need a . . . ," Grace began.

"A drink?" The policeman lifted her chin and looked into her face. He was a young black man with kind eyes. "Miss, it's none of my business if you want to ruin your life. I'll run you in when you get drunk and cut you loose when you pay your bail, and someday maybe I'll find you back under there dead. Or smashed up inside your car."

Grace shook her head. "I'm fine," she croaked.

The policeman took out a small black pad and a pen. He wrote briefly, tore off the sheet, and stuffed the paper in the pocket of her jeans. "That's the number for A.A. Alcoholics Anonymous. They meet every Saturday—" He checked his watch. "Well, you could make the meeting tonight. It's over behind city hall."

"I'm not an alcoholic," Grace tried to say, but her words were slurred beyond recognition.

"Your choice, miss," the policeman said regretfully. "But you get off the streets till you sober up. You sure as hell don't look any twenty-one to me, not that that stops anyone in this town."

He walked away, leaving Grace disoriented and confused. Lights were coming on all along the boardwalk. The sun was just a pale red glow behind the shops. What day was it? How long had she been passed out?

She stumbled up onto the boardwalk, pushing uselessly at her hair, stiff with sand and dried salt water. Her blouse was buttoned wrong, but the effort to straighten it seemed too great, and she gave up.

The one thing she was sure of was that she needed a drink. Needed it desperately.

A young couple brushed past her, and Grace caught a glimpse of the woman's look of disgust. She stumbled on as the feeling slowly returned to her legs. She made another attempt to straighten her blouse and this time succeeded. But the act of fixing the button brought on a flood of memory.

She stopped dead, covered her mouth with her hand, and stifled a sob. That couldn't have happened. It couldn't. It was just some nightmare she was confusing with reality.

She shuddered and shook her head to

clear away the images. But they came back, like a lurid, slow-motion film. She wanted to turn away, but there was nowhere to turn.

Tears wanted to come, but her entire body was dehydrated, too parched to cry. Her stomach rebelled, but nothing came up. Grace sank to her knees on the boardwalk, squeezing her eyes shut with the heels of her hands, grinding them, trying to scrub away the memories.

"Grace!" It was a shout from far away. She opened her eyes, looking about wildly. There, far down the boardwalk, was that Kate?

Not Kate. Kate couldn't see her like this.

Grace levered herself up and stumbled toward a side street, diving away from the incriminating lights of the boardwalk. She heard her name again and ran into an alley, knocking over a garbage can in her haste.

Halfway down the alley she stopped, gasping for breath, flattening against the building. At the end of the alley she saw Kate run up, then stop. Someone joined her. Justin.

"I'm sure it was her," Kate said.

"She may not want to talk to any of us right now," Justin said. "Officer Stigers said she was pretty out of it."

"I'll go after her," Kate volunteered.

Grace didn't wait to hear any more. She

slid along the grimy wall, careful to stay in the shadows, then ducked around the corner, stumbling, picking herself up, and lurching onward.

Her mind was a whirlwind, a merry-go-round of disconnected thoughts, horrible memories, and over it all a terrible need. She was sobbing, dry-eyed, with no destination or purpose. Was she going insane? Was that what this was? Her mind was no longer her own.

Then, across the street, looking the wrong way, she saw Chelsea. They were all after her! All trying to grab her, lock her up somewhere. She ducked behind a row of cars and crab walked along, oblivious to the outright expressions of disgust, even anger, from people on the street.

"There she is," a voice sang out, and she broke into a run, arms pumping, feet falling unevenly on broken pavement. Her heart was racing. Her lungs burned. She fell against a parked car, slid to the dirty pavement, and gasped for air. Running feet passed by and faded away.

She saw a pair of old, varicose-veined legs standing before her. A woman in a long, dowdy dress and clunky shoes. She looked up at the woman, an old woman with her hair tied back in a bun, a big carpetbag over her shoulder.

"I need a drink," Grace whispered.

The woman bent down and took Grace's arm, lifting her to her feet. "I know you do, child."

"Will you help me?" Grace asked.

"I will."

The woman took Grace's arm and led her, sobbing, across the parking lot. Grace knew she would help. She could feel it. The woman understood. She understood.

They were climbing a set of wooden stairs, up to a landing. A young man stood there, holding a door open. He looked at Grace and smiled shyly at her.

He understood, too, Grace realized. It was all going to be all right. They would get her a drink, she would have a chance to think, to sort it all out, to realize those memories were really nothing but nightmares. . . .

The woman led her inside, to a room filled with people, all sitting on folding metal chairs. At the far end of the room was a podium, brightly lit.

Grace collapsed into a chair, covering her face with her hands. She wanted to die. She wanted it all to be over. She wanted the memories gone. She heard a cry of despair and realized it was her own.

The old woman patted her on the back. "I know, baby," she said softly. "I know."

The room grew silent and expectant. There was a stir near the front, and Grace opened one eye. A man was walking up to the podium. A dark-haired man in a leather jacket.

He turned to face the audience and began to speak. "My name is David," he said. "And I'm an alcoholic."

"Hello, David," the audience answered.

"I've been sober now for two years—"

David's voice faltered as he saw her. His eyes locked on hers, carrying unspoken volumes of information. He smiled at her. Then he went on. "I've been sober now for two years, but before that . . ."

Here's a sneak peek at

Making Waves #3: Sweet

one

"Ladies, I'm afraid I'm going to have to ask you to put your tops back on."

Justin Garrett stood with his arms crossed over his bare chest, feet planted firmly in the blistering sand. One of the two teenage girls splayed on the nearby beach blanket looked up at him, shading her eyes against the brilliant noon sun. She smiled and said something Justin couldn't understand, waving her hand expressively. The sweet smell of coconut suntan oil wafted toward him.

"There's no nude sunbathing on this beach," Justin said.

The second girl sat up. *"Qu'est-ce qu'il dit?"*

"Je ne comprend pas," said the first girl, shrugging.

French, or at least French Canadian, Justin guessed. Ocean City got a lot of Canadian tourists. Great. This was not a situation that could be handled intelligently with sign language. Justin gazed toward the water, carefully scanning his two hundred meters of shoreline.

When he looked back down at the girls, a shadow had fallen across them.

"Need a hand?" Alec Daniels asked, deadpan. Alec was a fellow lifeguard and a housemate of Justin's for the summer.

"I think I can deal with it."

Alec shook his head, fighting a grin. "I thought I'd better get a closer look at the problem."

"Yeah, I'll bet you did," Justin said. "This is *my* section of the beach, Daniels."

Alec pursed his lips. "I wasn't so sure. It looks to me like it's right on the line. And I didn't want to shirk my duties."

Justin looked back down at the girls, trying very hard to keep his eyes focused on their faces. Fortunately he was wearing dark sunglasses. "Does either of you speak English?"

"Non, je suis desolée," the first girl said, cocking her head. *"Nous sommes françaises."* Then, in a heavy accent, she added, "French."

"Great," Justin muttered. "You need to wear a top," he said, making a pantomime of picking something up with both hands and tying it in back of his neck.

Alec snickered. The girls exchanged mystified looks.

"Ils sont beaux, tous les deux, hein?" the second girl observed.

"She said we're handsome," Alec said. "Both of us. Although I'm pretty sure they were just being nice to you."

"You speak French?" Justin asked.

"A little," Alec admitted. "Two years in high school."

"Then tell them to put their tops back on," Justin said, exasperated.

"Do I have to?"

"It is the law. If we don't tell them, the cops will."

"What a shame." Alec sighed, then attempted an explanation in stumbling French.

After a moment the girls began retying their bikini tops, their rapid-fire conversation heavily punctuated by giggles and rolled eyes.

"What are they saying?" Justin asked.

"I'm not getting it all, but the general idea seems to be that we're immature and ridiculous, and that a man with any sophistication would be able to handle the sight of a woman's breasts."

"Wonderful," Justin said flatly. "I always like to make a good impression." He turned back toward his lifeguard chair, waving over his shoulder to Alec. "Later."

It had been a slow day so far. The surf was

breaking softly, and even the gulls, wheeling and dodging overhead, seemed less offensive than usual. There was a good crowd on the beach, but they'd been a well-behaved bunch by and large.

Justin kept his gaze on the water as he walked, taking note of everyone in his section. The old, fish-belly-white man staring out to sea and smoking a cigar as the waves lapped at his waist. The young boy trying out a snorkel and mask in too shallow water. The high school couple a hundred yards out, arms linked across an air mattress, kissing and laughing.

At the water's edge two little girls were taking Barbie and Ken on a date to a sand castle. A blond boy, seven or eight, hovered near the castle, no doubt plotting his demolition strategy.

Justin climbed back onto his white wooden perch. "Immature and ridiculous, huh?" he muttered. He grinned and once again began his methodical scanning of the water.

He heard a chorus of shouts and looked over to see the little blond boy launch a sneak attack on Barbie's sand castle. The boy raced off down the beach, the two little girls and their dolls in hot pursuit. He hadn't gone far when he slammed into the legs of a middle-aged man wearing a Dodgers baseball cap. The man laughed good-naturedly, and the boy sped on.

Justin returned his gaze to the sea. Something nagged at him, though. He glanced back at the man in the cap. He was wearing dark sunglasses; he was thin, not very tan, and long legged. And he seemed to be looking at Justin. Staring. Justin furrowed his brow, staring back. But the man's face was lost in the bright glare of the sun.

"Where's the nearest bathroom?"

The voice, coming from just below his chair, startled Justin. He looked down at a mother holding a squirming toddler in her arms.

Justin gave her directions, and by the time he looked back, the middle-aged man had vanished.

Making Waves Surf Camp Sweepstakes
Official Rules

1. **Entry:** NO PURCHASE NECESSARY. A PURCHASE DOES NOT IMPROVE YOUR CHANCES OF WINNING. VOID WHERE PROHIBITED BY LAW. Enter by filling out an official registration form (pursuant to Alloy's Privacy Statement and the Children's Online Privacy Protection Act (COPPA) located at the "Making Waves Surf Camp" page at http://alloy.com. , or if you want to enter by mail, see below. If you are not an existing Alloy member, you will be asked to register for a free Alloy ID through on-screen directions which shall request your first and last name, mailing address, and email address. Sweepstakes begins June 15, 2001, at 12:01 AM Eastern time and ends November 30, 2001, at 11:59 PM Eastern time. Automated or robotic entries submitted by individuals or organizations will be disqualified. To enter by mail, send a 3x5 card on which you have hand-printed your first and last name, address, telephone number and email address (if available) to: "Making Waves Surf Camp" Sweepstakes Mail-ins, 151 West 26th Street, 11th Floor, New York, New York 10001. All mail-in entries must be postmarked by November 30, 2001, and received no later than December 6, 2001

2. **Privacy:** By entering the Sweepstakes, you agree to Alloy's use of your personal information as described in Alloy Online's Privacy Statement at http://alloy.com/company/privacy/.

3. **Eligibility:** Only legal U.S. residents thirteen years or older are eligible to enter this Sweepstakes. Employees of Alloy Online, Inc. ("Alloy"), their respective parents, their affiliates, subsidiaries, suppliers, printers, distributors, advertising and promotional agencies, prize suppliers and the immediate family or household members of each are not eligible to participate or win.

4. **Winner Selection:** The winner will be selected in a random drawing from among all eligible entries on December 7, 2001, to be conducted by Alloy designated judges, whose decisions are final. Winners will be notified by e-mail, or mail as applicable, on or about December 10, 2001. Odds of winning depend on the number of eligible entries received. The Winner (or, if a minor, the parent or legal guardian) may be required to execute and return an Affidavit of Eligibility and Liability/Publicity Release within fourteen (14) days following attempted notification, or the winner may forfeit the prize and an alternate winner may be selected. Any winner notification returned as undeliverable will result in prize forfeiture and an alternate winner shall be selected. No prize substitutions or transfers are permitted.

5. **Prize:**

One (1) Grand Prize / A Trip for Two at Paskowitz Surf Camp in Southern California – Winner will receive a trip for the winner and one companion for five (5) days at the Paskowitz Surf Camp in San Diego, California during the Summer of 2002. Trip includes roundtrip coach airfare, accommodations and meals at the camp, ground transportation between the camp and the airport. Travel times shall be determined by Alloy. Winner is responsible for incidental expenses. Alloy reserves the right to substitute the prize for another prize of equal or greater value. APPROXIMATE RETAIL VALUE: $6,000.

6. **General Conditions:** This Sweepstakes is governed by the laws of the United States. All federal, state and local laws and regulations apply. All taxes, fees, and surcharges are the sole responsibility of the prize winner.

Except where legally prohibited, each winner (and parent/legal guardian if winner is a minor) grants (and agrees to confirm that grant in writing) permission for Alloy and those acting under the authority of each to use such winner's name and likeness for all advertising and/or publicity, without notice, review, approval, or additional compensation. Entrants further agree that Alloy, their respective parents, subsidiaries and affiliated companies, advertising and promotion agencies, suppliers, printers, distributors, and the respective officers, directors, employees, representatives and agents of each will have no liability whatsoever for, and shall be held harmless by entrants (and parent/legal guardian if entrant is a minor) against, any and all liability for any injuries, loss or damage of any kind to persons, including death, or property damage resulting in whole or in part, directly or indirectly, from acceptance, possession, misuse or use of any prize, participation in this promotion, or while traveling to, preparing for or participating in any prize-related activity. Alloy expressly disclaims any responsibility or liability for injury or loss to any person or property relating to the delivery and/or subsequent use of the prizes awarded. Alloy makes no representation or warranty of any kind concerning the appearance, safety or performance of any prize awarded. Restrictions, conditions, and limitations apply. Alloy will not replace any lost or stolen prize items.

7. **Conduct:** By entering this Sweepstakes, entrants agree to be bound by these Official Rules. The Official Rules will be posted at the Sweepstakes Site throughout the Sweepstakes. Entrants further agree to be bound by the decisions of the judges, whose decisions are final and binding in all respects.

8. **Limitations of Liability:** Alloy is not responsible for any incorrect or inaccurate information, or any technical or human error which may occur in the processing of submissions in the Sweepstakes or any damage to entrant or user equipment. If, for any reason, the Sweepstakes is not capable of running as planned or is affected by events which corrupt or affect the proper conduct of this Sweepstakes, then Alloy reserves the right to cancel, terminate, modify or suspend the Sweepstakes.

9. **Winner's List:** The name of the Winner will be posted at Alloy.com by December 10, 2001 and is available by mail after December 10, 2001, by sending a self-addressed, stamped, #10 envelope to: Alloy, 151 West 26th Street, 11th floor, NY, NY 10001, attn: "Making Waves Surf Camp" Sweepstakes Winner. Residents of Vermont and Washington may omit postage.

10. **Official Rules:** For a mailed copy of the official game rules, send a self-addressed, stamped envelope (residents of Vermont may omit return postage) before June 24, 2001 to: Alloy, 151 West 26th Street, 11th floor, NY, NY 10001, attn: "Making Waves Surf Camp" Sweepstakes Rules.

11. **Sponsor:** Alloy is the sole sponsor of this Sweepstakes and is responsible for the fulfillment of the Prize.